Praise for Kate Perry's Novels

"Perry's storytelling skills just keep getting better and

better!"

—*Romantic Times Book Reviews*

"Can't wait for the next in this series...simply great

reading. Another winner by this amazing author."

—*Romance Reviews Magazine*

"Exciting and simply terrific."

—*Romancereviews.com*

"Kate Perry is on my auto buy list."

—*Night Owl Romance*

"A winning and entertaining combination of humor and

pathos."

—*Booklist*

Other Titles by Kate Perry

The Laurel Heights Series:

Perfect for You

Close to You

Return to You

Looking for You

Dream of You

The Family and Love Series:

Project Date

Playing Doctor

Playing for Keeps

Project Daddy

The Guardians of Destiny Series:

Marked by Passion

Chosen by Desire

Tempted by Fate

Looking for You

Kate Perry

For my Magic Man's grandma Jeanne, who, after meeting me, turned to him and said, "Let's keep her." Regardless of her good sense and excellent taste, she's a legend.

Also to Parisa Zolfaghari and Julie Linker: Thank you. If you were here with me, I'd drown you in champagne (non-lethally), rub your feet with scented oils, and feed you delectable sweets (after I washed my hands).

And, lastly, smooches for my Magic Man, who tells me I'm great and encourages me to be even better, even when I threaten to defenestrate him. I love you, baby.

Chapter One

IT WAS A dark and stormy night.

Gwen chuckled as she slipped on her red rain slicker. Good thing she was an artist instead of a writer. If words were her livelihood, she'd be the proud owner of a cardboard box instead of a lovely store in Laurel Heights.

Checking the straps on her rollerblades, she rolled through her shop, Outta My Gourd, stopping once to rearrange one of the displays. It still boggled her mind that she'd built all this. Ten years ago, if someone had told her she'd end up a gourd artist, she'd have immediately taken the person to a psychiatric ward.

If her family knew how she made her living, they'd *definitely* lock her away. No de la Roche would *ever* consider being anything so common as an artist, much less one who painted squash. The paparazzi would have a field day.

Which was why she ran away and became Gwendolyn Pierce, anonymous free spirit.

It'd been the best decision she'd ever made, and she had her grandmother to thank for it. If Mamie Yvette hadn't encouraged her to leave the nest and find her own way, she'd be miserable and trapped instead of content and fulfilled. She'd come into her own. If Mamie Yvette could see her now, she'd wink in her sly way and ask how freedom tasted.

It tasted delicious.

It'd be perfect, if it weren't for the fact that she couldn't tell anyone who she'd been. *Anyone.* The more people who knew, the greater the chance of her secret getting out.

She stopped, hand on a light switch, and looked around her store. If her secret got out, she'd lose all this. She'd lose her independence and privacy. The media — she cringed, thinking what a zoo that'd be. Her friends would look at her differently, and she'd question anyone's motive who wanted to get to know her.

The very thought was crushing.

But sometimes she just wanted to be loud. She wanted to cause a ruckus instead of living quietly in the shadows.

She wanted to be seen, to be acknowledged—for herself, not because of her name.

She wanted to accept the de Young Museum's offer.

They'd called again today. They wanted her to participate in a special exhibit: "Artisans of the Americas: Past and Present." They asked her to do a modern gourd project inspired from one of the ancient gourds the museum had on display. Other artists were participating, and in the end one project would be picked as a permanent exhibit in the museum.

Just the thought of it made her want to jump up and down with excitement. How incredible would it be to have her work displayed in one of the premier museums of the world? Her grandmother would have been proud of her.

But there was no way she could do it.

She couldn't chance the recognition and attention it'd draw. What if someone recognized her as the missing Geneviève de la Roche and outed her?

She resented needing to hide.

Unfortunately, hiding was better than having to live under a microscope again.

Gwen flipped the lights off and went outside to face the unseasonal August storm.

Before, as Geneviève de la Roche, she wouldn't have been allowed to rollerblade at all, much less rollerblade in rain.

"Before no longer exists," she murmured to herself, locking the door.

The heavy click of the latch was like the past was shut behind her. Memories didn't always stay shut away, but the further she got from them, the more distant they seemed.

Distant was just the way she wanted to keep things, because there was no way she was going back. Not that her family would take her back, anyway.

Except Mamie Yvette. Her grandmother would welcome her with open arms, *chocolat chaud* waiting, wanting to hear of all the adventures she'd had over the fourteen years Gwen had been gone.

Over the years, they'd had intermittent contact — brief, unsatisfying calls from disposable phones and such — but it'd been fleeting and infrequent. When Gwen had settled in San Francisco, Mamie Yvette had asked her not to gamble her happiness and call again, afraid someone would discover her location. It'd been three years since their last conversation.

She missed Yvette de la Roche.

Gwen shook off the melancholy that blanketed her whenever she thought about her old life and stepped into the storm. Holding her arms open, she embraced the rain and let it wash her thoughts away, focusing on the little things she appreciated so much — the crinkly sound of the slicker, the feel of the water weighing down her grown-out curls and running down her neck, the anticipation of the hot bath she'd have when she arrived home.

Carefully, she pushed off down the slippery sidewalk. She hadn't gone two blocks before a car slowed to a snail's pace next to her.

Normally, she'd have ignored it and sped away, but it was the sort of car she'd always wanted: one of those old American tanks, restored to its original glory. Even in the deluge she could see the gleam of the dark paint and the fancy rims. She slowed down, admiring the beauty.

The window rolled down. Gwen started to smile automatically, but then she saw the driver's face and her smile faded, replaced by a jittery feeling in the pit of her stomach and sweaty palms. For some reason, being around Rick Clancy always did that to her.

Of course he did. He was a private investigator,

and she was a woman with a secret.

He leaned across the bench seats and scowled out the window at her. "What the hell are you doing?"

"Going home," she said, wanting to smack his handsome face. Not that she'd *ever* admit she found his dark, mysterious looks intriguing.

That chiseled, manly face looked at her now, the same way it always did: with distaste. "It's raining," he said as though she were five.

"No wonder you're a private investigator." The rain stopped feeling invigorating and began to chill her. She drew her coat closed tighter around her neck. "You're so astute."

He studied her with sharp eyes. "Only someone insane would rollerblade in this storm."

She shrugged, knowing it'd irritate him. "No one ever accused me of being sane."

"Get in."

She blinked in surprise. "You're offering me a ride?"

"Yes." He sounded like it pained him, too.

"Why?" she asked suspiciously. They didn't get along. They hadn't from the moment their mutual friend, Olivia, had introduced them to each other.

She thought he was overbearing and bossy, and he considered her to be loony. Not that she cared what he thought — much. "You don't like me."

"I don't trust you. There's a difference."

She stepped back from his probing gaze. He was too observant, and she had a past she didn't want anyone to uncover. The last thing she needed to do was jeopardize the new life she cherished by getting friendly with someone who made his living ferreting out people's secrets, no matter how attractive he was.

"I don't trust you, either," she said finally.

"Good, it's unanimous." He leaned forward. "Look, I'm only offering the ride because if Olivia finds out I let you trek home in this she'll be pissed. You know Olivia."

Olivia Parker-Wallace was the closest friend she'd ever had. Being from such a wealthy family, Gwen hadn't had many friends growing up. It was hard to be close to people when you constantly questioned if they liked you for yourself or for your family name. Her brother Roger was kind, but he was so much older they'd never really been friends. She hadn't had anyone except her grandmother.

That was one of the reasons she'd bonded with

Olivia so quickly and completely. Olivia had grown up with her grandmother, too. Plus they were both shopkeepers in Laurel Heights. Olivia's lingerie store was just down the block from Outta My Gourd.

Gwen hadn't known Olivia long, but she knew Olivia had opinions, one of them being that she and Rick were meant to be together. So, yes, Olivia would have insisted that Rick give her a ride home.

Of course, Olivia didn't know of Gwen's past, or that hanging around a private investigator was the last thing she needed to do. She shook her head and said the one thing that was guaranteed to send Rick running. "Olivia thinks you and I should date."

His expression didn't change. "I wonder why that is."

"I'm a catch. She thinks I'd be good for you."

"Is that what you think?"

She thought she wanted to strip him naked and pour chocolate all over his body. But how idiotic would it be to invite a detective into her life? "What else could it be?"

"Maybe *I'm* the catch."

He *was* a catch—she'd always thought so, even if she'd never verbally admit it. Successful, highly educated, and settled. Funny and smart. As if that wasn't lethal enough, he was long and lean and hard, nothing soft or pampered about him. Every time she saw him, something in her went tingly and reckless.

It annoyed her.

So she laughed at his statement. By the look on his face, it'd sounded genuine enough to deceive him. Then again, why wouldn't it? She'd been taught to hide her thoughts and feelings behind a facade before she could even walk.

Rick glared at her. "Look, my upholstery is getting wet. Just get in the goddamn car."

"I'm capable of making it home on my own."

"I don't care. I'm giving you a ride."

"Why?"

He leaned out the window. "Get. *In.*"

The glare on his face should have frightened her, but oddly she felt a shiver of excitement, very similar to the feeling she'd had the day she'd run away. Excitement mingled with a touch of fear and the knowledge that her life would never be the same from that day forward.

"Ridiculous," she murmured. Getting a ride from Rick was nothing like running away from her family.

"It *is* ridiculous," he growled. "We're both getting

soaked, and you're standing there like a stubborn fool. For the last time, get in the goddamn car."

Hell no, she thought as she opened her mouth and said, "Okay."

Chapter Two

He'd lied.

Rick gripped the steering wheel, very aware of the woman sitting next to him. He'd told Gwendolyn Pierce that he offered the ride because Olivia would be pissed at him if he hadn't, but that wasn't true. Yeah, Olivia would nag him about it, but she'd let it go after two seconds. Really, he'd offered Gwen the ride because he couldn't help himself. It'd been clearly a moment of insanity.

He glanced at her. She stared ahead, seemingly oblivious of the rain dripping down her face. Her big blue eyes were clear and lucid, which he found odd: he'd known artists and they tended to live in an altered state most of the time. She wore one of those red rubber raincoats little kids wore, and somehow she made it look sexy instead of silly. On her lips, she wore a dreamy half-smile.

He wanted to kiss it. Bad.

Which showed how insane he really was, because if there was ever a woman he shouldn't lust after, it was Gwendolyn Pierce. He stole another glance at her. What color was her hair this week? The last time he'd seen her it'd been a sick shade of pink. Today it had red and orange stripes in the crazy curls. Even with her hair wet, the streaks looked interesting. Pretty, like a sunrise. She used to look like a psychedelic Shirley Temple, with her rainbow curls, and since her hair had grown out past her shoulders, she looked...

Kind of sexy, actually.

But it was still weird. Weird was the perfect word to sum up Gwendolyn Pierce. Shaking his head, he said, "You should drive on days like this."

"I don't have a car," she said in her surprisingly husky voice, "and even if I did, I wouldn't be able to drive it because I don't have a license."

He stopped at a red light and faced her. "How is that possible?"

She shrugged. "I've never needed one."

"Everyone needs a driver's license."

"So nosy people like you can use the info to stalk

me?" She tipped her head, brow arched. "The light's green."

He stared at her, not sure which urge was stronger: to spank her or kiss her. He would *not* think of doing both at the same time. He returned his attention to the road and focused on getting her home, wherever that was.

As if reading his mind, she said in her bedroom voice, "You haven't asked me where Narnia is."

Gripping the steering wheel, he glanced at her. "Narnia?"

"My flat." She looked at him with those waif eyes that could make a man drop to his knees and promise the world. "I named it Narnia, because when you step through the front gate you enter a magical realm. It's the perfect artist's *atelier*."

"Atelier?" He arched his brow. She said the word in a perfect French accent.

"Attic. Workshop. Whatever." She waved a graceful hand.

"Sure, whatever."

"Go onto Masonic and turn right on Page," she instructed. "I'm up a couple buildings on the next street, Ashbury, just below Haight."

The upper Haight was a high rent area, and Laurel Heights had some of the most expensive retail areas in San Francisco. How did an artist afford one of those places, much less both? "Do you have roommates?" he asked.

"No."

"Don't tell me people actually buy those vegetables you paint."

She faced him. He didn't look at her, but he could feel her glare across the seat in the dark. "They're gourds, and my work is quite fine, I'll have you know."

"They look like hollowed-out, deformed pumpkins." Actually, one time Olivia had dragged him into Outta My Gourd and when no one was looking, he'd examined one of the gourds. The painting on it had been exquisite. Not that he'd ever admit that.

"They aren't deformed pumpkins. They're art," she declared proudly. "In fact, the de Young museum has asked me to participate in a show they have coming up. 'Artisans of the Americas: Past and Present.'"

Impressive. "That makes sense. Pumpkins are an early American thing."

"They aren't pumpkins, but I guess I shouldn't

expect you to have an educated view on art."

"Why not?" He'd studied criminology, but he'd taken an art history course one semester, mostly to meet girls but he'd been surprised that he'd enjoyed it.

"Because you're so blue collar."

Even he had to grin at that. "Does that intrigue you? Is the princess attracted to working class men?"

Gwen stiffened. "Don't call me that."

Princess? He wanted to ask why not, but then she turned on him. "Why did you offer me a ride? You obviously don't like me, and Olivia wouldn't have known if you'd driven right on by. So why are you doing this?"

Agitated, her voice almost sounded like it had an accent. It was faint, but he'd bet his PI's license he wasn't imagining it. It had a French lilt to it. "Because you were rollerblading in the rain."

"So?"

"So it's crazy. Who does that?"

"I do." She stiffened. "I do whatever I please. I don't have to answer to anyone anymore, much less you."

Who did she answer to before? A man? And why did it bother him so much that there may have been a man that she'd been beholden to? He shouldn't care one way or the other.

He cleared his throat. "It's not safe. Rollerblading at night is bad enough, especially given the areas you're going through, but in the rain with the way people drive in this city, you're liable to get yourself killed."

"San Francisco is one of the safest cities I've been to in the world. I'm not sure why you care anyway."

Neither was he. He tried another tactic to get information out of her. "What's the least safe city you've lived in?"

She gave him a baleful look.

Those eyes were lethal. He shook his head and kept his gaze forward. "You must have gotten everything you wanted as a little kid."

"Not hardly."

"I would've bet Lance that you were pampered as a kid."

"Lance?"

"My car."

She snorted. "Because you're being nice to me and giving me a ride home, which I didn't ask for, by the way, I won't make any comment about Lance.

But don't cars usually have girl names?"

"Feeling Lance's power, you can't possibly doubt that he's all male." He patted the console.

"Men and their toys."

He saw a smile flirt with her lips and got lost in a carnal daydream involving her lips and a certain part of his anatomy. He cleared his throat. "You were telling me about your childhood."

"No, I wasn't." Her smiled faded. She crossed her arms and stared out the window.

Not a happy childhood, then. But in what way? Was her family tough on her, or was she an orphan? He'd ask Olivia, except she'd take it to mean that he was interested in Gwen and he didn't want to open that can of worms.

So he tried another tact. "I bet your parents hate that you rollerblade late at night."

Next to him, Gwen wilted, drawing into herself, looking small and cold, like an orphan.

Christ—maybe she was. He felt a wave of remorse and the urge to take her in his arms and offer comfort. Before he could say anything, she pointed to the left, across the intersection, and said, "Pull over there."

He did as she asked, putting the car in park. Then he faced her.

She shook her head. "I don't want to hear it. You gave me a ride, I'm going to thank you, and then I'm going up and taking a bath."

The image was instant: her, soaking in a large tub, her toes peeking, her body obscured by a million bubbles. An unruly part of him grew a little too interested.

"So, thanks." She grimaced a smile and opened the door.

He reached out and grabbed her sleeve, startling both of them.

Gwen blinked at him with her amazing eyes. "What?"

Before he could stop himself, he leaned across the seat and kissed her. Her lips were soft. They were innocent. And *hot*.

He stilled, looked at her with her eyes wide like a caught deer, and knew he was a goner. With a groan, he tangled his fingers in her hair and lifted her mouth to his.

She took him, less with finesse than eagerness. She scorched him with her lips, the promising flick of her tongue, her greedy hands teasing his skin and hair.

Something woke inside him, roaring to life, urging him to take her. It was as unexpected and startling as it was exciting.

She sat back, her lips glistening, her eyes wide with the same shock he was feeling. She swallowed audibly, her gaze on his mouth. Then without a word, she got out of the car, closed the door, and rollerbladed to the next building.

Rick sat and watched her put in a code for the gate. He waited until she was inside, until he couldn't see her any longer.

He gripped the steering wheel to keep from running after her. That was a bad idea. Gwendolyn Pierce was the last woman on earth he should want. She was hiding things.

But the way she kissed...

He shook his head. He couldn't go there. Yet.

He'd been a PI for too long. He lived by his instincts, and they were screaming that something didn't add up.

Gwen didn't add up.

Who was she?

He sat in the car, blown away by her presence. He made it a point not to check up on people that he knew. It was too easy to get caught up in the distrust that went hand-in-hand with being an investigator. Everyone hid something. Everyone had secrets.

Gwen set off his alarms though. Big time.

He'd check up on her. A little. Chances were he wouldn't find anything.

He didn't believe that in the slightest.

Chapter Three

CHAOS WAS NOT Camille's friend.

Phones ringing, people shouting over short gray cubicle walls, printers constantly spitting out pages... She was surprised more reporters didn't go postal.

She huddled in her un-ergonomic work chair and tried to focus on the article she was supposed to turn in that afternoon. She stared at her ancient monitor and the Word document displayed on it. She only had one paragraph—not a good one at that. She kept trying to bring excitement to the beekeeping phenomena swarming San Francisco, but she wasn't succeeding.

She wasn't sure she could be blamed.

"Bernard!"

Wincing at the strident yell, she cautiously stuck her head up over the walls of her "office."

Her boss stood in the doorway of his office—a

true one, with real walls and a door. He waved a paper at her impatiently. "Get your butt in here, Bernard."

Sighing, Camille stood up and tugged her skirt straight. She grabbed a pad and pen for notes and went to see what torture Mac Murray was going to inflict on her next.

Mac didn't look up from his keyboard when she walked in. "Close the door," he barked, pecking out letters with his index fingers.

How an editor could have such poor typing skills, she didn't understand. Watching him was painful. She figured that was the reason Mac looked like a caricature of a newspaperman. The comb-over, disheveled stained button-down shirt, and paunch hanging over his belt made him appear legit.

She sat in the chair across from his desk and waited for her next assignment, wondering what it was going to be. An exposé on school lunches? The plight of San Francisco's sea lions? The astronomical number of souvenir sweatshirts sold to tourists every year because they didn't expect the weather in the city to be so cold in August?

Camille shook her head. Those weren't mundane

enough. Mac had a gift for giving her the dullest topics known to mankind.

"Bernard," Mac said, pushing his keyboard aside, "I want you to write an article about feng shui."

"Seriously?"

"No, I'm just kidding." He rolled his eyes exaggeratedly. "Yes, *seriously*. It's the sort of crap people care about in San Francisco. That and recycling."

She told herself to feel lucky that she wasn't asked to write about plastic bottles. "Is that it?"

"No." Mac shoved around stacks of paper, obviously looking for something. "I also want you to cover the new exhibit at the de Young. It's something about local artists' take on relics of the Americas."

That sounded moderately interesting. "Okay."

"They've asked some artists to participate, but you'll have to find out who has and who hasn't. I have the names of some of the potentially participating local artists." He held up a page, triumphantly. "Here."

She took the notes and stared at them. "A rug weaver? A *gourd artist*?" She hated this job.

"Yeah, whatever the hell that is." He reached for his keyboard. "Interview them. The museum's director, too. Get on it as soon as you turn in your feng shui article."

If she were her mother, the Pulitzer Prize winning journalist Elizabeth Bernard, she'd throw the pages back in Mac's face and demand a decent assignment. Something important, like teenage crack whores on San Francisco streets, or corruption in the city government. Her mother wouldn't even *touch* a fluff piece on rugs and gourds. Her mother would give her that steely look and tell her to grab her nuts and demand what she wanted.

Elizabeth was often disappointed in her.

Camille cleared her throat. "I can do both of these, Mac, but maybe I could also do a bigger article, maybe something about — "

"No." Mac leveled a stare at her. "Look, Bernard, I know you're looking for a big break, but this is the way to syndication. You pay your dues with these articles and you'll make it to the big time."

"Like Leona James?" she asked with more sarcasm than she usually let leak out. She couldn't help it. Leona had told her she'd been fed the same line of crap that Mac was trying to get her to swallow. Only now it was twenty years later, and Leona was still covering stories about seagulls at the Giant's ballpark. It put Camille's five years here at the paper in harsh perspective.

Mac frowned at her. "Are you sassing me, Bernard? You know there are plenty of hungry kids out there who'd love to have your job."

"No," she backtracked quickly. "No sass. I'll get on this story right away."

"Good." He waved at her dismissively and grabbed the phone. "Get the hell out of my office."

She stood stiffly and walked out. The second she stepped into the open office space, her ears were assaulted by all the ringers.

She hated the phones most of all. She cringed each time a shrill ringer sounded as she wove through the rat's maze of cubes.

In a perfect world, she'd have her own office, gently lit with indirect sunlight and no noise except for Bach whispering through computer speakers. One time, she'd gone through the office after everyone had left for the night and turned all the ringers off. It'd been a whole blessedly quiet day before anyone had realized.

She returned to her desk. Not ready to face the beekeeping article again, she pulled out her cell phone. There was a text from Dylan, saying he was at Four Barrels in the Mission and that she should join him for a writing date.

She loved seeing Dylan. He was one of her best friends—really one of her only friends. They'd met at a book signing right after she'd graduated. She'd gone because the author was a former professor of hers and Elizabeth had told her she should go network. Dylan had gone because he'd been dating the professor.

Dylan was an author, as well. A bestselling thriller writer. When they'd met, they'd bonded over Stephen King, mini quiches, and their mutual dislike critics. They'd become friends, getting together for occasional writing dates and to go to readings. Even when he and her professor broke up, they kept up their friendship. It was nice.

Only lately he'd been nagging her more and more about her writing. It made her want to avoid him, and that made her sad because she liked seeing him.

She started to text back *Can't—thanks*, but today, the thought of staying and working made her want to pull out her hair, so she grabbed her purse and headed to BART.

A Colma-bound BART train pulled up as she stepped on the platform. She rode it to 16th Street, hopped off, and walked the few blocks to Dylan's favorite coffeehouse.

Dylan was seated in the window, like always, laptop open, brow furrowed over his latest manuscript. Sometimes she teased him that he looked like Hugh Grant, with the way his brown hair flopped on his forehead, knowing being compared to the pretty actor irritated him.

In reality, Dylan was much more attractive than Hugh Grant. She knew because she'd met the actor when her mother had interviewed him a number of years ago.

She headed to him and set her purse down on the counter. "Hey."

He looked up, smiling in that way that lit his entire being. "Hey, yourself. You got here fast."

"Anything to get out of the office."

"Hold that thought." He slid off the stool and reached into his pocket. "I need another espresso. Mocha?"

"Please." She watched him walk to the counter to order their drinks.

The women around them did the same. She couldn't blame them. Dylan was a catch. A serious rock climber, Dylan was chiseled all over. Once she'd slept on his couch and in the morning he'd walked out in nothing but boxers, so she could attest to his hotness firsthand.

But being hot wasn't what made him so appealing. He had a magnetism that drew people. Well — female people, anyway. Put a bag over his head and that wouldn't change. He had a way of looking at a woman like she was the only person who existed in that moment.

Being in his scopes was a heady thing — except she knew they were just friends. He'd never tried anything with her. She wasn't sure why — maybe because she was nine years younger. Or because she wasn't his type. He dated sexy, confident women who ruled the world.

Camille didn't rule anything.

After she'd gotten over the annoyance of being defined as a friend, she'd been glad for it. It was better this way.

He came back to their spot, placing her mocha carefully in front of her.

Taking a sip, she sighed. "I needed this. Work was getting to me today."

"Work is always getting to you," he pointed out.

"It was worse today. Mac wants me to interview a rug weaver and a gourd artist."

Dylan blinked. "Gourd?"

"Exactly."

"Have you tried telling your boss you'd like to try different assignments?"

"Yes. I asked today. He basically patted me on the head and told me to behave like a good little girl." She pouted. "I'm so frustrated. I'm tempted to tell him to jump off a bridge, but I need this job."

"Why?"

It was her turn to blink in confusion. "What do you mean, why?"

He shrugged. "Why do you need it? Take a sabbatical and write a book. You've always wanted to."

Not this again. Her hand tightened on her cup. "I want to be a journalist."

"No, that's what Elizabeth wants." He stared at her with the grounded gray gaze she was so familiar with. "What about the book you started after college, when we first met?"

"What about it?"

"Maybe you should start working on that again."

"No." The book had been a mistake. Just the thought of pulling it out and working on it made her freeze on the inside.

"Why not? You're not happy at work, and you're a great storyteller." He nudged her leg with his. "You know I don't say that to just anyone."

It was true. He was brutally honest when an aspiring writer asked for his critique.

But her mother didn't agree. Five years ago, Elizabeth had found the beginning of her manuscript. Camille hadn't realized until she found the marked up pages on her bed. The pages had bled red ink. The one comment that stood out was SUPERFICIAL written in bold block letters across the first page.

She shook her head. "I'm not a fiction writer. Besides, I have a salary and benefits at the paper."

"I know you don't think so, but you'd be more successful doing what you're meant to do. Happier too."

That was debatable, and Elizabeth certainly wouldn't make her life easy if she decided to quit journalism.

"Just think about it, Camille." Dylan downed his espresso and set the cup aside. "Ready to write?"

"I didn't bring my laptop or notebook." To counteract the obvious disappointment in his expression, she said as brightly as she could, "I just wanted to see you. It's been so long. How's the book coming?"

"Slowly. My deadline is sneaking up and I feel like I'm trying to herd cats."

"You always say that. Then you pull off a miracle and turn in a bestseller. I'd hate you if I didn't love you so much," she joked.

He didn't smile, instead watching her in that intent way of his. Normally she ate it up. This time, it made her squirm. Finally he said, "If you loved me, you'd listen to me and write more. For yourself, not for the paper. You'd find your true voice."

She withered at the disappointment she heard in his voice.

She was used to her mother being frustrated with her. Camille didn't need to spend tens of thousands of dollars in therapy to know that she was going through all these hoops at work to get Elizabeth's approval.

But having Dylan disappointed in her was jarring, and it happened more and more. He seemed like he was losing patience with her, but she didn't know why.

She'd figure out what to do about it, though. She'd make him proud. Elizabeth too. She was smart—she'd figure out how to do the impossible.

"I need to get back to my chapter." Dylan gestured to his computer.

"I have to get going anyway." She downed the rest of the mocha and stood up, trying not to feel hurt at being dismissed. "I have to finish my article."

"Okay, sure. Whatever." He shrugged.

She wanted to assure him she'd make it up to him, but actions were stronger than words, and she didn't know how to act. So she walked out, feeling worse than she had at the office.

Chapter Four

"WHAT ARE YOU drawing?" Laurel said as she pulled out a chair and sat down next to her.

Gwen hadn't even realized she'd been drawing anything. She'd come in to the Purple Elephant, the children's art foundation she'd started a couple years ago, hoping volunteering would get her mind off Rick and the way he'd kissed her.

No such luck. That kiss dominated her thoughts. She sighed. "Nothing, really. I was just doodling."

"That's really good for a doodle."

She studied her sketch. Apparently, the kiss dominated her drawing too. The couple she'd drawn was locked in a passionate embrace. It was different than her usual work—more elegant, more abstract, more passionate. She'd never done anything like it.

Laurel was right. A shiver ran up Gwen's spine, the way it did when she knew something was *good*.

It'd be perfect for the de Young.

Not that she was going to accept the commission—no matter how much she wanted to.

"I couldn't draw that if I meant to," Laurel continued.

"That's not saying much." Gwen tugged the girl's ponytail. "You *did* fail art."

The teenager rolled her eyes. "Isn't it against some teacher code that you're not supposed to harass students?"

"I'm not a teacher, and you come here of your own will." Laurel had come to the Purple Elephant at the beginning of the summer because she'd failed her eighth grade art class. Her dad, a creative type, considered it important that she learn to draw. Laurel couldn't even draw a stick figure.

But the girl could do anything technological, so Gwen had put the girl to work redesigning the Purple Elephant's website. It was a win-win for everyone, except Laurel's father, who still thought his daughter was taking drawing classes. Gwen had wanted to tell him the truth, but Laurel had begged her not to.

So Gwen kept her mouth shut. She understood the strain of parental expectations and needing to live your own life.

Laurel pursed her lips as she looked at the drawing from another angle. "Are they having sex?"

"What do you know about sex?"

"I'm fourteen," she said, as if that explained it all.

It was Gwen's turn to roll her eyes. "Have you ever even been kissed?"

"Yes. Last year." She frowned.

"It doesn't look like it was a good kiss."

Laurel looked at her like she'd just exclaimed that she was from Mars. "It was *awesome*. But he doesn't skate, and when I tried to teach him he fell and scraped his elbows. He hasn't talked to me since."

Gwen brushed a lock of hair back from the girl's face. "Then he didn't deserve you."

"He really didn't," Laurel agreed matter-of-factly. "But it was just as well, because we only had two things in common, and everyone knows you need at least four things in common with someone to make it work."

"I didn't know that."

"Yeah, but you're kind of clueless." The teenager wrinkled her nose apologetically. "I mean, sorry, but you can't deny it. When was the last time a boy kissed you?"

Last night, she wanted to brag—and it was awesome, too. Goose bumps rose on her arms, thinking about it. He was like one of the heroes her author-friend Lola wrote about in her romance novels. Masterful. Confident. Hot.

She wasn't used to feeling like this—the aching deep in the pit of her belly and the restlessness. She'd had crushes, and she'd had a couple boyfriends, but it'd been a long time. Frankly, it was hard being intimate with someone when you had to hide your past. Lately, she'd been so focused on establishing Outta My Gourd that she hadn't thought about dating at all.

Not that she was thinking about dating Rick. She just wanted to handcuff him to her bed and have her way with him.

Did private investigators have handcuffs?

"Earth to Gwen." Laurel knocked her arm. "Has it been *that* long since a boy kissed you?"

"Like I'm going to tell you."

"Because it was probably during the eighties."

"I was a child in the eighties."

"That's what I'm saying." Laurel shook her head. "Seriously though, you should date. You're pretty and smart. A guy would totally tap that."

"Thank you. I think." Why had *Rick* kissed her? What did the kiss mean? He didn't like her. At least, she'd never thought he did.

Now she had doubts. You couldn't kiss a person you didn't like—not like that. She'd felt that kiss all the way to her toes and back. Not even her bath had been able to relax after Rick's kiss. She'd gone to bed, agitated and disturbed.

Yearning.

"Only you have to be careful who you hook up with because you don't want to be miserable." Laurel's young face looked strained.

Gwen had the urge to soothe the worry from it. Laurel had mentioned once that her parents were fighting at home. That sort of thing weighed heavily on everyone in a household, especially a teenager. Her own parents had never fought, but Gwen understood strain.

"So you need to ask the right questions," Laurel said in all her adolescent wisdom. "Like if he likes opera."

"Opera?"

The girl nodded. "If you like opera and he doesn't, it'll just make you guys fight. You'll want him to go

43

with you but he'll say that's three hours of his life he'll never get back, and then you'll get made and make him sleep on the couch."

Gwen blinked. "That's harsh."

"No kidding."

"I don't like opera."

"Good." Laurel nodded in approval. "Make sure he doesn't either."

She tried to picture Rick at the opera, hunched in a small seat without nearly enough legroom to accommodate his long legs. But she could picture him in a tux, eating her up with his darkly intense gaze, secreting her into a dark corner and kissing her until her toes curled.

She cleared her throat. "So what else do I need to find out?"

"If he's a vegetarian, because you'll get pissed if you want to make a steak for dinner and he just wants spinach."

Gwen made a face. "Gross."

"I know, right?"

"But I don't cook."

"That's good then, unless he doesn't cook either. Then how will you eat?"

"Take out?"

"Good point."

Gwen laughed. "You've thought about this a lot."

Laurel shrugged. "I want to be prepared if I ever meet someone."

"Good decision. Thanks for the advice." Not that she needed it. She planned on staying away from Rick Clancy. He wasn't interested in *her*—he wanted to ferret out her secrets. It was in his DNA to need to solve a mystery. "How long are you going to be here today?"

"As long as I can." Laurel made a face. "My mom's working from home today."

"Ah." Gwen soothed the girl's back. "It's hard, isn't it?"

"Tell me about it." Shaking her head, Laurel hopped up and went to check on one of the younger kid's drawings.

Gwen watched Laurel. The first time she'd seen the girl, she'd recognized the look in her eyes—the need to live up to her parents' ideal of her. She'd instantly decided to take the girl under her wing, but sometimes she wondered if it wasn't really Laurel who looked after her.

Glancing at her sketch one more time, she packed up her notepad and put the charcoals away. On her way to the office in back, she chatted with some of the children she'd gotten to know over the summer. She needed to go open her store — it was already past noon — but she always took time for the kids.

Besides, on her rollerblades, it didn't take long to get to Laurel Heights from the Mission. Twenty-five minutes, more or less, from where Purple Elephant was located to Outta My Gourd.

The real benefit to rollerblading: it gave her an outlet to get rid of some of her naturally over-abundant energy. The tai chi master she'd met years ago in Oregon had shown her how to channel and calm her "restless chi," as he called it.

Of course, back then she'd had good reason to be restless. She'd been constantly looking over her shoulder, waiting for the paparazzi to swoop in and smother her.

She hated the media. She had since she'd been six when they'd labeled her the Grape Princess because she'd shown up to a press conference with jelly on her face.

That picture had followed her into adolescence.

Worse: her father had punished her for making a mockery of the de la Roche name. She'd felt embarrassed and shamed. And guilty, because her favorite nanny had been fired for not making sure she'd been presentable.

To this day, thinking about it made her tense.

But she didn't have to deal with the press any longer. She'd done a good job disappearing, changing her name and appearance. She'd become Gwendolyn Pierce, bohemian. No one connected rainbow-haired Gwen to the missing Grape Princess. She doubted even her mother would recognize her if they were in the same room.

Of course, her mother probably wouldn't recognize her regardless. Being a parent hadn't been high on Janine's list of priorities. Why would she trouble herself with a dirty job like mothering when she had a team of nannies at her beck and call?

"That's the last thing I need to think about right now," she said to herself as she bladed up Sacramento Street. Talk about getting agitated.

To distract herself, on impulse she rolled into Grounds for Thought. A croissant, and then she swore she'd open the store.

It was past the noon rush, but Eve's café was still

busy. Eve was a natural marketing whiz. Gwen had learned a lot from her in the time they'd known each other.

Actually, if it hadn't been for both Eve and Olivia, she'd have been floundering. They'd taken her under their wings and shown her how to be a businesswoman. Olivia had been the one who'd introduced her to Rick.

And Rick had kissed the breath out of her last night.

"Don't go there," she muttered as she wheeled in. She skated over to the counter, where Olivia was talking to Eve. "Can anyone join?"

"No, but you're not *anyone*." Eve smiled in welcome, tucking her sleek blond hair behind her ear. "You look flushed. From rollerblading?"

"Yes," she lied as she gave Olivia a hug. Under no circumstance was she telling them she was blushing from X-rated thoughts about Rick—or that his kiss had rocked her world. Especially since it was never happening again.

Her friend held her out at arm's length. "You look different."

She put her hand to her lips. Did it show? It wouldn't surprise her—she still felt the press of his mouth to hers. "I changed my hair color last week," she offered hopefully.

"Why are you blushing like that?" Olivia studied her shrewdly. "You look guilty."

"Maybe she had a rendezvous with a man," Eve joked.

Gwen's face burned hotter.

"Oh. My. God." Gaping, Olivia set her coffee mug down. "You *did*. Is that where you've been all morning? Who is he?"

"No one. If I'm flushed, it's because I just came from the Purple Elephant." Then, for good measure, she improvised with, "And I'm excited about a new project."

"A new series of gourds?" Eve asked.

Thinking about the drawing she'd inadvertently done at the center, she nodded. "I think it'll be a hit."

The women exchanged a look.

She laughed. "No, I'm not planning another Jerry Garcia tribute. You made me see it wasn't such a great idea."

Eve smiled. "It was mostly the giant tie-dye inflatable gourd on your roof that we thought was a mistake."

Not all her ideas were winners, but at least she tried. Her grandmother had taught her that. *Try everything, Geneviève*, Mamie Yvette used to tell her. *Grab life by the tail and hold on tight. It's a grand adventure.*

"What's this new idea?" Olivia asked.

She shook herself out of the past. "Something different." Impulsively, she added, "The de Young Museum asked to include me in an exhibit. They want me to do a gourd series inspired by the gourds of the early American natives. I sketched a design that'll work nicely for it."

"That's amazing." Eve's eyes lit up, and it was obvious her brain kicked in with all the possibilities. "That'll put you on the map. Just think of all the good PR that'll result. I'll help you send out press releases."

Olivia nodded. "Make sure it's part of your contract that they'll sell some of your gourds in the museum gift store. It'll get your name out there."

She swallowed the flare of anxiety at the idea of publicity. She wanted the recognition for her artwork, but she didn't want notoriety. "I haven't accepted the offer yet."

Both women frowned but it was Olivia who spoke. "You have to accept. How is this even a debate? How many artists get a chance like this?"

She nodded. "I know, but..."

"There is no *but*." Olivia stared at her. "What's going on really?"

Before she could reply, the front door jingled, signaling someone's entry. She glanced over her shoulder and froze as Rick strode toward them.

Actually, it was more of a prowl than a stride, the gait of a jungle cat stalking prey. At that moment, based on the way his dark eyes were eating her up, she guessed she was the prey.

The tingling in her lips started again. Nerve damage? She swallowed and pressed her fingers to her mouth.

"Am I interrupting a coven meeting?" He gave Olivia a kiss on the cheek but kept his gaze on Gwen.

Her feet slipped from under her and she had to catch her balance on the counter. Now that she knew how devastating those lips were, she was shocked that Olivia didn't crumble to the ground.

Olivia gave her a quizzical look. "You okay, Gwen?"

"Sure," she squeaked. She rolled away some more, just in case. "I need to get going."

"But you haven't gotten anything yet," Eve said, her brows furrowed in concern. "A croissant like usual?"

Coming in for one of Eve's croissants was part of her morning ritual. She loved them—they were the best she'd had this side of the Atlantic. They reminded her of the croissants their cook Jean-Marie used to make for her and her brother, Roger, fresh every morning. "Yes, please."

"And chai?"

"Yes, to go." She hated coffee, not because of the taste but because her father had drunk coffee. The smell reminded her of the way he'd criticized all of them, especially her, first thing every morning. Of course, now she understood why he was hardest on her, and, frankly, she couldn't blame him. It couldn't be easy to find out your child wasn't biologically yours, especially for a man like Gautier de la Roche.

That was her family's skeleton in the closet. The de la Roche's were excellent at keeping secrets.

"You haven't been in your store all day," Rick said. He sounded casual, but she could tell he wasn't. Why was he looking for her?

To kiss her again?

Right, Laurel would say. He probably hadn't given their kiss any more thought. So she arched her brow coolly, trying to show how unaffected she was, even though she was anything but. "What are you accusing me of?"

"Only guilty people are paranoid," he retorted.

"Children," Olivia chided mildly. "Mind your manners."

Gwen pointed at him. "He started it."

Rick snorted.

Eve handed her the croissant and chai. "It's on me, this morning, Gwen. A pre-celebration for you accepting the offer from the de Young."

"You're doing it?" Rick asked, crossing his arms.

His tone set her teeth on edge. He obviously didn't believe in her talent. She lifted her chin. "I'm still thinking about it."

"She's doing it." Olivia gave her a stern look. "You'll call them and accept when you go back to your shop."

Eve turned to Rick. "You know about Gwen's offer from the de Young?"

"I'd heard about it," he replied carefully. "It seems like a long shot."

Gwen rounded on him, sloshing some of the chai on her hand when her skates got away from her. Shaking it off, she glared at him. "Just because you don't understand art doesn't mean the people at the museum won't either."

"Princess, if pumpkins were art, then Halloween would be year-round."

She rolled to him and poked a finger in his chest. "You're an imbecile."

"You're—"

"I'm doing it," she declared brashly, poking him again just because she wanted to feel his chest. Firm. He must work out. "And I'm going to win the honor, and then you'll eat your words."

"What's going on with you guys?" Olivia looked back and forth between the two of them. "I don't know whether to give you time out or to send you to a room to work out the tension."

Gwen's gaze shot to Rick's. He was remembering last night too—she could see it in the way his dark eyes heated up. Her breath caught in her chest, and she swore her lips began to throb. Her creative mind pictured being in a room with him all too well.

The image made her so flustered, the only words

that came to her were in her native French. She had to breathe and calm herself before she could say, in English, "I wouldn't enter a bedroom with him if my life depended on it."

"And yet you took a ride from me last night," he countered.

"Because you wouldn't leave me alone!" She turned imploringly to Eve and Olivia. "He all but forced me into his car."

Her two friends goggled at her.

Olivia was the first to recover. "You gave Gwen a ride home, Rick?"

He scowled. "She was rollerblading home in a torrential downpour. Who does that?"

"Me." Gwen lifted her chin proudly. "I've been completely on my own for a long time and doing just fine. I don't need anyone to take care of me."

He snorted again.

She narrowed her gaze. "I'm going to prove you wrong about the museum, you know."

"Princess, if your pumpkins win, I'll eat one."

"I'll start looking up recipes for you then." With a cool nod at Eve and Olivia, she bladed out of Grounds for Thought. She'd show him.

She stalled for a moment, thinking of the press, but she shook it off. No one would put together that funky, bohemian Gwendolyn Pierce was really Geneviève de la Roche, the Grape Princess. There was no reason to connect her with the wine heiress she'd once been.

She'd show him. She'd show everyone. She'd show the world who she really was.

Chapter Five

Like every evening at Durty Nelly's, his favorite Irish pub in the city, it was hopping with the regulars who poured in after work. Usually, Rick chatted with them while he waited for his buddy Treat to arrive. Tonight he stared unseeing at the untouched pint before him.

He couldn't get that woman out of his mind.

Gwendolyn Pierce, a walking contradiction. Artist who lived in a gentrified neighborhood. Businesswoman with expensive overhead. Free-loving hippie chick who kissed like it was her last night on earth.

Established shop owner who didn't exist beyond seven years ago.

"Hey." Treat pulled out the bar stool next to him. "You just get here?"

"No."

Treat arched a brow at the beer. "Are you as love-sick as Eve believes you are?"

He recoiled. "What?"

"She and Olivia are operating under the assumption that you're jonesing for Gwen Pierce." Treat signaled the bartender.

"That woman is a menace."

"I've always thought she was sweet."

"Sweet? *Gwendolyn Pierce*?" He snorted.

"She seems eccentric from what I've seen. It takes a special person to make a go at selling gourd art. But Eve likes her, and Eve is a good judge of character." Treat nodded to the bartender who pushed the beer toward him. "But you're a sound judge of character, too. Do you think there's something wrong with her?"

"What *isn't* wrong with her?" Lifting his Guinness, he took a hefty gulp. Then he said, "I ran a background check on her."

"Uh-oh."

"What does that mean?"

"Remember Brandy Welles in college?"

Hell yes, he remembered Brandy. She'd been tall, blond, and endowed. "What about her?"

"You ran a background check on her too." Treat

arched his brow. "You found out that she'd been adopted, only she didn't know until you told her."

"I have more finesse now."

"I know you were born into being a private investigator, with your dad in the business. I'm just saying that maybe you need to be less suspicious of people."

It was in his blood. There had never been any question about what he'd do once he graduated from college. The only way he'd defied tradition was by moving to San Francisco from Boston. His mom still chewed him out over that. "I'm not suspicious of people. I just have a healthy caution for what they say."

Treat grinned. "Uh-huh."

"And Gwen doesn't add up. Gwendolyn Pierce has only existed for the past seven years. There's no record of her before then. No school records, no college."

"She's an artist. A lot of artists don't go to college."

"But there's no record of her even graduating from high school. It doesn't make sense. She's educated. You can tell from the way she speaks."

"You're looking at this the wrong way," Treat argued. "She doesn't have a criminal record either, right?"

"Not as Gwendolyn Pierce." He leaned forward.

"She lives on Ashbury, close to Haight."

"Nice neighborhood. Perfect for an artist."

"But not an artist who doesn't have money."

"Doesn't she make money at her store? Rent is expensive in Laurel Heights. She wouldn't be able to survive there long without turning a profit."

"Exactly. But she has two steep rents: the store and her apartment. Based on her taxes, she's making good money, but not enough to cover both rents."

Treat groaned. "You checked her taxes?"

"It's all part and parcel."

Shaking his head, his friend said, "You're over-thinking this. Her apartment is probably rent controlled."

"She's only lived there two years."

Treat stared at him incredulously. "Why do you care?"

"I'm curious."

"This goes beyond curiosity. This borders on obsession."

Ever since he kissed her, he *felt* obsessed—and he didn't like it. "She's not what she seems. If you listen closely, sometimes she has a little bit of an accent."

"What sort of accent?"

"French."

"Gwen is the least French of any person I've ever met." Treat leveled a serious look at him. "Maybe you should back off and leave her alone."

Rick wished he could do that, but that was like telling the moth to leave the flame alone. He had to know.

Sliding off the bar stool, he downed a swallow of beer and pushed the rest across the countertop. "I should head out."

"So soon?" Treat asked. "You haven't even finished your pint."

He didn't have the patience to sit there long enough to finish it. He felt antsy in a way he didn't understand. So he stood and dropped enough money to cover their drinks on the counter. "Go home to your woman. I'll see you later."

Treat grabbed his arm before he could leave. "You aren't going to do anything stupid, are you?"

"Would I do that?" He clapped a hand on his friend's shoulder and walked out.

Normally, he walked home from Durty Nelly's. He owned a house just four blocks away. Tonight, he headed that way, only as he approached the driveway and saw Lance parked there, he bypassed the front door and headed straight to his car.

Just a quick check, he told himself as he pulled out.

It was past nine in the evening, long past the time all the stores were closed. Meaning Gwendolyn was probably already ensconced in her Narnia.

"Narnia." He shook his head as he turned onto Lincoln Avenue and headed toward the Haight.

Since there was no available parking on the same block as her apartment, Rick drove up the street a couple blocks until he found a spot. Locking Lance, he put his hands in his pockets and strolled toward her home.

What was he doing? This was insane. Treat was right—Rick was entering stalker territory. Being paid to hunt down information on someone was one thing; doing it because you couldn't help yourself was quite another.

He blamed Gwen. She was an enigma. Contradiction upon contradiction. Heaven and hell in one package.

"I'm definitely losing it," he muttered, looking at the outer gate to her building.

As if conjuring her, the gate swung open and she walked through. Head down, she closed the gate and walked down the street away from him.

Irritation surged through him. She didn't even look around to see if there was anyone else on the street. Where was her sense of preservation? What if he were a thug, out to mug her? Or worse?

And what was she wearing? He squinted, trying to see in the dim streetlight. Not even she would wear a robe out in public, would she?

But that was exactly what she had on: a short robe with bare legs and, seemingly, nothing on underneath.

That wasn't an image he need in his head.

Drawing himself in to be less conspicuous, he followed her. She turned left and walked down to another couple buildings before she stopped and peered through the bars of a gate.

Who was she going to visit? In a robe? With—he squinted—a towel around her neck?

"Booty call?" he asked himself. Feeling a wave of anger, he stopped behind a tree and waited to see who'd come out to meet her.

He never expected her to scale the iron gate and

drop inside the yard, showing a whole lot of pale leg in the process.

Shaking off the shock, Rick hurried toward the gate and peeked in, just in time to watch her skulk around the corner to the back of the house. He looked at the gate, then back at where she'd disappeared, and shrugged. Grabbing the spokes at the top, he anchored himself on a foothold and hauled himself up and over.

He landed on his feet, jarring his knees. Cursing under his breath, he hobbled down the path Gwen had taken. The other half of the path branched to the front porch, which led to an ornate Victorian entrance.

It looked like a single-family house — a rare thing in San Francisco, where most of the old houses had been renovated into flats. When these old Victorians were kept intact, it was because the original family still owned them or because someone rich had bought it from the original family.

Did Gwen have a sugar daddy?

The thought disgusted him. Picturing an old guy touching her, siphoning off her youth and vitality for himself...

Rick wouldn't stand for it.

He stopped where the path ended, where the backyard began. Hiding next to the house, he peered around the corner.

The backyard was lush with greenery. There was a cushion-covered bed to one side, draped with gauzy curtains and stacked with pillows. Unlit tiki torches stood at intervals all over. Through the thick canopy of trees that protected the backyard from being viewed by neighbors, there was the thinnest glimmer of moonlight.

It reflected on the surface of the pool. He looked at it at the same moment he heard a gentle splash.

Gwen. He could see her silhouette, skimming under the water like a mermaid. She came up for air and then submerged again, like she was born a water creature.

She stopped suddenly, bobbing in the center of the pool. "Are you going to lurk all night?"

He shrugged and stepped out from the shadows. "How did you know I was here?"

"Did you really think I wouldn't notice a large man following me on an empty street?" She wiped the water from her eyes and looked at him. "What are you doing here?"

"I was about to ask you that." He walked to the edge of the pool and squatted down. "This isn't your place."

"You really are brilliant at your work, aren't you?" she asked sarcastically, treading the water.

He stayed silent, watching her. Waiting.

She heaved a sigh. "This is my friend's home. She's gone most of the time but she lets me use her pool."

She. The relief was instant and staggering. Later, he'd analyze it. For now... "If she lets you use her pool, why do you have to break in?"

Gwen frowned. "I didn't break in. I hopped the fence."

He arched a brow.

"I couldn't find my key."

Instinct told him she was telling the truth. His dad had taught him the value of listening to instinct, and he never doubted his. But it was tempting to start now. "So you walk here in your robe and go swimming?"

"Pretty much."

"At night? In the cold?"

"It's heated. Do you think I'm crazy?" She shook

her head. "Don't answer that. I know exactly what you think of me."

That she was a temptress? What other explanation was there? She turned him on despite himself, no matter how hard he tried to resist her. She was trouble and he should run away, but there he was, standing by a pool at night, wondering what she looked like in her swimsuit. "I think you should come out."

"Why?" She smirked at him. "Are you going to arrest me, Officer?"

"Is that a veiled way of asking me to cuff you?"

Her eyes widened but she turned her head so her face was obscured. "You *would* take an innocent comment and turn it into something sordid."

"Princess, there's nothing innocent about you."

"Don't call me that." She ducked into the water, a glimpse of creamy skin before she disappeared under water. She surfaced at the edge and hauled herself out.

Water sluiced down her body, but it didn't distract him from the view. He'd have expected her to wear some old-fashioned, granny-style swimsuit—an ugly one-piece at the very least.

She wore the tiniest bikini he'd ever seen. Bright

yellow. Small triangles pieced together by string. Lithe body, slim shapely limbs. A whole lot of wet skin.

"Holy..." he said, trying not to swallow his tongue. He gave himself props for not drooling visibly.

"What?" she asked suspiciously, grabbing the towel she'd left at the side of the pool.

He waved at her, head to toe. "It's a crime against nature to hide that under the hideous clothes you wear."

"If that's a compliment, you need to work on your delivery."

He wasn't sure what it was. All he knew was that he felt like he'd been clobbered over the head.

She picked up her robe, shaking it out before she slipped it on. "I don't know why you're so stuck on proving that I'm nefarious, but you're wasting your time."

"You're hiding something." The least of which was that killer body. He pushed his hands deeper into his pockets. They were safer there.

"Everyone hides things." She pointed at him. "You just assume everyone has dark secrets."

"In my line of business, everyone does have dark secrets."

"Your business sucks." She yanked the sash of her robe tight and walked past him. "Creating gourd art may be different, but at least I'm adding something beautiful to the world."

Before he could figure out what to say, she lifted her elfin chin and said, "I entered my art in the contest at the de Young. I'm going to win."

When she said it like that, he believed her. Still, he couldn't help goading her. "It's a long way to winning the coveted spot in the museum's permanent collection."

She leaned toward him. "Want to bet that I'll win?"

A drop of water trailed down from her wet hair into the vee of her robe. He wanted to follow it with his tongue, burrowing his head in her chest and inhaling her scent. She'd smell like teenage summer — of chlorine and innocence. His chest ached with need and something unfamiliar.

"Well?" she said, poking him in the middle of his chest, where he felt the weird ache most. "How about a bet?"

He shook off the ache and focused. "What stakes?"

"A hundred dollars if I win."

"A hundred bucks?" He'd been thinking along the lines of a kiss—deep, passionate, and encompassing, maybe with a little groping. A hundred bucks was a lot of money for most people. He'd think doubly so for an artist with two expensive rents. He frowned, feeling that nagging suspicion that something about Gwen didn't add up. It eclipsed some of the arousal he was feeling.

Oblivious of his doubts, she gave him a cocky smile that made him want to wrestle her to the ground and kiss her. "You losing confidence?"

Confidence was the least of his problems. Gwen was the main one, and he was determined to figure out what she was about. So he stuck his hand out. "You've got a deal."

Chapter Six

*T*HE BED WAS heavy.

Camille tried setting her weight against it, but it wouldn't budge. Maybe if she took the mattress off?

She shoved it off the ancient wooden frame, propping it against a wall. She anchored her feet against the wall, with her butt on the frame, and pushed.

Nothing.

Dropping to the floor, she sat there and wondered what to do.

She could not move her bed. But she'd been reading up on feng shui for that article she needed to turn in at the beginning of the week, and she realized that her career was in tanker because her living space was completely wonky. Her helpful friends spot was a mess of dirty clothes, her relationship corner held a paper shredder, and there was absolutely no prosperity anywhere to be found.

No wonder she'd been struggling so much at work.

She thought moving things around might help. It certainly couldn't hurt.

But her bed was being difficult. And if she couldn't move her bed, there was no way she could move the behemoth dresser.

Not by herself, at least, but if she called someone like Dylan then it'd be a piece of cake.

Okay, maybe she was looking for a reason to talk to him. The way they'd left things the last time had left a bitter taste in her mouth. She didn't like feeling like she'd disappointed him.

Impulsively, she picked up her phone and called him.

"Camille," he said when he picked up.

On his tongue, her name was like a caress. She knew they were just friends, so she'd never go *there*, but she hoped one day she met someone else who'd make her feel the way he did when he said her name. "Dylan, I need help."

"Should I come to you, or do you want to come here?" he said without preamble.

It was one of the reasons she loved him. She

clearly aggravated him to no end, but he still showed up—without question. "Come to me. I'm at home."

"Okay."

"What are you wearing?"

She could hear the grin in his voice. "Shouldn't that be my line?" he asked.

"No, I need some manual labor help, and I don't want you to come over in, I don't know, a suit."

"I wear suits so often. I'll see you in fifteen." He hung up.

She quickly put away the rest of the clothes she had laying around. She put away the romance novel she had on her nightstand—it seemed like incriminating evidence, somehow. She found one last pair of pink panties when the doorbell rang.

Stuffing the panties in a random drawer, she ran down the stairs to open the door for Dylan.

He stood on the porch, leaning in the doorway, wearing jeans and a T-shirt, looking like every woman's dream.

He was her friend, she reminded herself, because she didn't have more to offer him than that. Pasting a smile on her face, she waved him inside. "You got here quickly."

"Maybe I was eager to see you." At her incredulous look, he chucked her under the chin. "You're right. The serial killers in my books are prettier."

"I've read your books, so I know it's true." She grinned. "Come upstairs. I need help."

He followed her up the stairs. "Where's Elizabeth?"

"Out." Otherwise, she wouldn't have been able to invite him over. When her mother was at home, she was working, and when she was working, you didn't disturb her unless you wanted to suffer the consequences.

"Nice," was all Dylan said. Then he stepped into her room. "Did we have a hurricane in San Francisco, and I didn't notice?"

"I'm writing an article on feng shui, so I decided to test out its principles."

"Are you going to redecorate in squash when you interview that gourd artist?"

She gave him a baleful look.

"So what does feng shui say about a room in shambles?" he asked, looking around.

"It's in transition, not in shambles." She frowned at the bed. "I couldn't move it."

"Where do you want it to go?"

"In my creativity bagua."

He grinned. "I don't know what a bagua is, but I don't think anyone can find fault with wanting to inspire more creativity in bed."

"*No.*" Her face flushed hot. "That's just the position I want it in."

"I know." He winked at her and then became all business. "So where are we moving things?"

She showed him, and they began shifting things around. It wasn't easy—even with the extra brawn, the furniture was still heavy.

But they did it. The whole while she tried not to notice that Dylan had way too many muscles for a writer.

She failed.

When they had everything arranged, she surveyed the room. "I like it, actually."

"Good." Dylan collapsed on the bed. "Because I wasn't moving things again without serious incentive."

"Like?" she asked as she dropped on the bed next to him.

He faced her, turning on his side with head

propped on a bent arm. "Dinner."

"Is that all?" she asked, rolling towards him.

"Does that mean you'll have dinner with me?"

"As long as we go to McDonald's." She grinned ruefully. "I can't afford more than that on my salary."

He tugged her shirt. "Maybe shifting your room will make you realize you're meant to do bigger things than write and bees, furniture, and squash."

"I realize it. I just need the world to recognize as well."

"So about dinner," Dylan said, crossing his arms. "I'll pay, so we don't have to go to McDonald's. Absinthe?"

Camille sighed. She *loved* Absinthe. The bar was old-fashioned and the food was delicious. Most of all, Dylan knew how much she loved the restaurant, which had to be why he picked it. "I think I could probably manage to get away from my busy schedule for dinner."

"Good." Dylan smiled that intimate smile of his that made women melt.

She averted her gaze—just enough—because she wasn't impervious. "When?" she asked, pretending to be occupied with a corner of her bedspread.

"Let me check my schedule. I'll call you."

She nodded.

"Camille?"

She looked at him.

He held up a pair of black thongs.

"*Give me that.*" She snatched them out of his hand, her face crimson.

"Wear those to dinner and I'll make sure you get dessert." Chuckling, he strode out of her room.

Camille stared after him, confused, listening to his footsteps on the stairs. What had just happened? She's moved the paper shredder out of her relationship corner—maybe the results were immediate?

No. Shaking her head, she hurried after him. He'd probably just had too much caffeine.

Chapter Seven

$\mathcal{R}$ICK HUNCHED OVER his desk, looking at the file he'd compiled on one Gwendolyn Pierce.

It didn't look good.

On the surface, she looked legit, but that was the surface. Underneath? There was no underneath. She had no driver's license or passport. It appeared that she'd opened her first bank account and began establishing credit seven years ago.

If she was in the witness protection program, it'd explain everything. But she wasn't—he'd checked with a good friend of his at the bureau. Which left one of two possibilities: she was on the run from the law, or she was hiding to avoid being hurt by someone.

He didn't like either option.

Leaning back in his executive's chair, he studied the tiles of his office's ceiling. Not for the first time he thought he should post a picture up there to stare at when he needed to think. A centerfold would be in line with the stereotype of a private eye.

It was important to maintain a certain seediness when you were an investigator, otherwise your clients didn't believe you were competent. TV had done bad things for PIs.

So he cultivated that image. His office was located in Chinatown, on the third floor, above a hole-in-the-wall dim sum joint and a "massage" parlor. He had leather furniture, nice but slightly worn, and he made sure his cleaning lady kept the office just messy enough to make him look authentic but not like a slob.

It worked for him.

Turning to his computer, he did a Google search on Gwendolyn, expecting to find her website and other gourd related material. To his surprise, there was only one listing for her: purple-elephant.com.

He snorted as he clicked on it. *Purple Elephant* sounded just like her.

The site was for an art foundation for kids, in the Mission. Rick scanned through the site, surprised when he found out that Gwendolyn Pierce was one of the founding members.

He frowned. He wouldn't have expected it.

Actually, she was nothing like he expected. Where he'd assume she'd be flighty, she was dependable—he'd called the Purple Elephant and found out that she came in regularly, several times a week. Where he'd guess that she'd be unfocused, she was the complete opposite. You had to be to run a business so successfully.

It didn't compute. *She* didn't compute.

A quick call to the Purple Elephant, and he discovered she was volunteering until six that evening. Glancing at the time, he grabbed his jacket and went to check it out.

Parking across the street, Rick slumped in his seat and watched the front entrance of the foundation. He knew this was crazy. He knew he shouldn't have been there.

He assured himself he was running surveillance on Gwendolyn because he had nothing better to do. If he had a case that was pressing, he wouldn't be there. If he had a date, or if he needed to do laundry, he wouldn't have been skulking in the Mission, waiting for a curly-headed artist to emerge from a large purple building.

Rick knew he was lying to himself.

As if on cue, his subject rolled out of the front door, a bright flare of color. She wore orange skinny jeans with a dark green jacket that matched her rollerblades. The ends of an orange and pink scarf fluttered behind her. She slung a beat up burgundy messenger bag over her shoulder, lifting her hair out from under the strap.

All the colors should have looked ridiculous, but they were perfect on her. There was a quirky smile on her lips, and her gleaming curls bounced in happy tandem with her glide. He knew the sunset-colored corkscrews were soft to the touch and her lips sweeter than he could have ever predicted.

She wasn't anything like his type. He usually went for tall, curvy, elegant women. Women who inevitably bored him after a few months. He couldn't keep his eyes off Gwen. He felt like he could look at her forever and still be surprised.

A tall, skinny girl followed her out the door, holding a skateboard. Gwen joked around with the kid for a few minutes, surprisingly chummy, before they went their separate ways.

His gut tightened with worry as he watched

Gwen maneuver around a couple walking. Those damn rollerblades. He wouldn't be surprised if he learned she'd broken her neck one of these days. Where was her helmet?

Oblivious, she skated down the street, fluidly zipping around people, waving to the occasional passersby as though she knew them. A light turned yellow, and instead of stopping she darted faster through the intersection.

He clenched the steering wheel. Didn't the woman have any sense of self-preservation? He waited at the light, knowing he'd catch up to her. His gut told him she was headed home so, worse case, he could take a different route and be there waiting.

Assuming she didn't make a stop or have plans with anyone.

He frowned at the image that popped into his mind, of Gwen having dinner with another man. He didn't like it. Moreover, he especially didn't like that the image upset him.

He caught up to her a few blocks away and followed her the rest of the way up Valencia, to Market and Franklin, and then left on Hayes. He stared, disbelieving. Was she really going to skate up Hayes and its monster hill? There were flatter ways of getting home.

But she did, proving that she was either crazier than he thought or had legs of steel. They hadn't looked *that* strong the night by the pool when he saw them bare.

He'd only replayed the entire scene a million times in his mind over in the past few days.

Mostly he thought about the way she looked in that little yellow bikini. And he thought about stripping it off her.

Knowing she was headed home, he took a different route and arrived before her. Luck landed him a parking spot directly across the street. He wedged his car in and slouched in the seat, waiting for her to show up.

She darted around the corner and up to her front gate. He watched as she punched the security code and opened it.

What he didn't expect was for her to turn around and crook her finger at him.

He blinked, stunned. *Caught*. He never got caught, and she'd done it twice.

She put her hands on her hips, her posture showing she was put off by waiting. Then she threw her hands in the air and called out, "You might as well come in."

And then she rolled into the courtyard.

He knew that if he missed the gate before it closed, he'd lose his opportunity, and he was dying to see where she lived. One day his insatiable curiosity was going to get him in trouble.

So he hurried out of the car and got to it in time.

The gate closed softly behind him. A long, dimly lit brick-lined walkway led to a garden and a set of stairs. On the bottom step, Gwen sat unbuckling her skates.

"You know stalking is both creepy and illegal, don't you?" she said without looking up.

"It's not stalking. It's surveillance."

She glanced at him as she took off her other rollerblade. "Did someone hire you to spy on me?"

"No." He walked up to her. "Professional curiosity."

"You can't help yourself?"

Her eyes looked large and luminous from this angle, and his gut clenched with want. "It seems not."

"Bummer. You might at least consider doing it in

a car that doesn't stand out so much." She picked up her skates and started up the stairs. "Come on."

He followed her up a million steps to the top floor. Plants encroached on the stairwell, and he had to duck in a couple spots. "I didn't know I'd need a machete."

"I'll lend you one." At the top, she opened a door and held it open for him. "Welcome to Narnia."

He looked around as he walked in. The apartment was sparsely furnished, but the few pieces she owned were good quality. A luxurious wide, low couch, a coffee table of wooden elephants holding up the glass top. Vibrant unframed canvases on the walls.

Clean and tidy. He shook his head, not understanding how his first impression of the woman could have been so off. "This isn't what I expected."

"What did you expect?" she asked, setting her rollerblades by the door. "Gourd seeds littering the floor? Used condom wrappers on the table? Red lights and filmy curtains?"

Something like that. "Am I so predictable?"

She laughed as she padded to the couch and curled into the corner. "Predictable is the last thing I'd call you."

"It's not a word I'd use on you either." He watched her rub her arches and tucked his hands in his pockets to avoid temptation, staying where he was, which was far away. He noted that the flat smelled fresh and clean. He took a deep breath, trying to catch a whiff of patchouli or incense or something, but he only smelled a hint of lavender.

Gwendolyn didn't fit the mold he expected her to be in, and he didn't like it. Staring at her, he said, "You're not who you seem."

She stilled for the briefest moment. It was such a minute change that he wouldn't have caught it if he hadn't been so engrossed in watching her. "Who am I?" she asked finally.

"I don't know, but I'm going to figure you out."

Her nose wrinkled with irritation. "I don't understand why you're doing this. You can't possibly be so bored in your work that you have to find pet projects."

The trace of French was in her voice again. He studied her, trying to find it in her, but she didn't look French. She looked like a fairy—a wood sprite. She certainly acted like one, believing in pixie dust and magical places. "Where are you from?"

She heaved a sigh. "What does it matter? You don't like me."

He nodded. "I didn't think so either."

"What does that mean? You've changed your mind?" Frowning, she set her feet on the floor, sitting up as though ready to bolt. "You can't possibly be that desperate."

"Desperate?" He stepped forward and pulled her up and against him. He knew the moment she felt the start of his erection, pushing against her belly, by the way her eyes widened. "Right now, desperate seems like the perfect description for how I'm feeling."

She swallowed audibly. "This doesn't make sense. We hate each other."

"I know." He brushed a curl from her face, tipping her head back and running his hand down her neck. He felt the wild beating of her pulse under his fingertips.

"This is mad," she whispered, answering his question by pressing her hips to his.

"Absolutely insane." He lowered his head and lightly bit the cord of her neck, right below her pulse point.

She moaned softly, her legs going weak. "Then

why are we doing it?"

"Because we can't help ourselves." He lifted his head and kissed her.

Chapter Eight

THEIR LIPS TOUCHED and Gwen forgot everything. Who she was. Where she'd come from. That Rick annoyed her. That she was flirting with danger by inviting him into her home.

Danger was delicious.

He walked her backwards a step so the backs of her legs hit the couch. Catching her as she tipped backwards, he eased her down and followed on top.

She gasped at the feel of him, surrounding her, warmer than her favorite cashmere blanket but not nearly as soft. One leg pressed between hers, touching her where she hadn't been touched by another human being in longer than she cared to admit.

It jolted her—with excitement *and* alarm.

She grabbed him by the hair and tugged. "What are you doing?"

"If you can't tell, I need to work on my technique." He lowered his head again.

She pulled him back. "You've been following me for days."

"Yes." He reached his hand between them, up her abdomen to cover her breast. "But I'm here now."

It was exciting, the slow way he rolled his hand over her. She couldn't help arching up even as she put a hand over his to stop him. "Are you seducing me just to weasel your way in and uncover my secrets?"

"I'm going to uncover your secrets regardless." He nuzzled her neck. "I'm seducing you because I can't help myself."

She arched her neck. "So what's happening here is a lack of control?"

"No. My control is excellent. What's happening here is desire." He rubbed her nipple as his knee pressed her right *there*. "It's want. It's necessity."

Starbursts erupted behind her eyelids, and she gasped at the electric feel that shot through her body. She wrapped her legs around him, savoring the way he felt against her. "We need boundaries."

"Fine, no whips." He tugged at her shirt to nibble her collarbone.

Who knew that bony thing was an erogenous zone? "Not that kind of boundaries."

"Whips are okay then?"

She pulled his head back again, frowning into his eyes. "You sound much too hopeful about whips."

"You're the one who brought them up."

"I did not."

Sighing, he sat back, straddling her leg. "You're not going to focus until we settle this, are you?"

"No."

"Okay, tell me your boundaries."

She opened her mouth to list them, but she had no idea what to list.

He grinned. "Do you need help, Princess?"

"That's the first thing. No calling me princess."

"I didn't know you were so into rules."

"I'm not." In fact, she hated rules. She'd grown up bound by them. She delighted in the fact that she didn't have to live by any anymore. "But this is different. I don't trust you, and if we're going to do this we need to establish some sort of parameters so I know what to expect."

"You can expect bone-melting pleasure."

"Really?"

"Really." He looked at her steadily. "Would it help if I promised I won't snoop while we're together? In or outside your home."

"Is it physically possible for you to turn it off?" she asked doubtfully.

"I think you can sufficiently distract me from professional matters." He traced a line down her neck.

She shivered, the tips of her breasts taut in anticipation. "And just to be clear, you expect to be around here more than just this evening?"

"I have a feeling this one evening isn't going to be enough to work you out of my system."

"So we'll just have sex until we've gotten over it?"

"Yes."

"And you're going to stop investigating my background while we're involved."

"I'll shift my investigations to your body," he said, his gaze running hungrily over her. Then he met her eyes again. "But no lying to me."

"I don't lie." She saw the disbelief in his expression, but she shrugged it off. She didn't lie — she just didn't disclose all the truth. "And this arrangement is temporary, lasting until we stop seeing each other?"

"Yes."

She nodded. "That seems like a fair agreement."

He studied her. "You don't seem upset by the temporary nature of this."

"It always works that way." She shrugged. "I get bored eventually. It's good to know that you're the same way. It saves on the drama when it's over."

His gaze narrowed, but he didn't say anything for a long time. Finally he asked, "So we've come to terms?"

Needing to ground herself, she lifted her chin. "I feel I should just reiterate that you irritate me."

"Good, because you irritate me too." He lowered his mouth to hers and gave her a kiss that went a long way toward melting her bones, just like he promised.

She was breathless and aching when he eventually came up for air. "This couch is very comfortable."

"Thank you," she replied politely, rubbing herself against him.

"It'd probably be more comfortable if we were wearing fewer clothes."

"Okay." She folded her arms behind her head and nodded. "Go ahead."

Rick arched an eyebrow. But then he sat up and stripped off his leather jacket, tossing it aside. His shirt followed, leaving his chest bare.

She licked her lips. He was defined, lean and sinewy. She wanted to run her hands along the muscles, but she kept her hands where they were, lowering her gaze to the thin arrow of hair that led to the waistband of his jeans.

He put a hand on his belt and slowly pulled it from the loops, letting it drop to the floor. He unzipped them, and where they gaped open she could see dark underwear and the hard ridge of his erection pushing against the fabric.

She licked her lips. "Are you stopping?"

"Pausing." He sat back on his heels, giving her space. "It's your turn."

She sat up eagerly. She shrugged out of her sweater, threw it aside, and wrestled out of the shirt she had on underneath. Leaving her camisole on, she moved on to her socks.

By the way he'd looked at her in her swimsuit, he liked her body, so she let him get his fill of her in that lacy camisole. Then she reached for the hem and pulled it over her head.

"You're not wearing a bra," he said, sounding strangled.

"You're so astute. Your detective classes have really paid off."

"No classes. I learned from my dad."

She looked at him, curious. "Your father is a private investigator too?"

"And his father before that. It runs in the family."

"Interesting." Greed ran in her family. And selfishness. Fortunately, she'd managed to escape without either trait.

He tugged on the waistband of her pants. "Take these off too."

She wiggled out of her pants, adding it to the pile of their clothes. She heard him swallow audibly. Hiding a satisfied smile, she leaned back and let him look his fill.

"You don't wear underwear at all?" he finally said, still not touching her.

The desire burning in his eyes excited her. This waiting was part of the game he wanted to play, and she was fine with that. It felt thrilling, and she wanted to revel in it. "Not usually. Now that Olivia and I are friends, I do sometimes. She's always giving us lingerie from her store."

"Please." He closed his eyes. "I'm already on sensory overload. I don't think I'll make it if I start picturing that."

She grinned. "I have this fabulous red lace—"

Covering her, he stole the words from her mouth with his lips.

The slide of his body against hers was luscious. She moaned as he surrounded her and filled all her senses. Wanting more, she touched him all over, feeling his muscles tensed, poised to pounce. She hooked her legs over his and held him as close as he could be with his pants still on.

He uttered a muffled curse against her lips, reaching down to fumble with his jeans. She slid her hand into the back, over his firm butt, as he finally pulled whatever he was looking for out of his pocket.

A condom. Seeing it made her want to rip his remaining clothes off—*now*. "Hurry," she urged him.

Groaning, he got up, shoved the rest of his clothes off, put on the condom. He was back on her, sliding in her, a second later.

She hadn't had sex in a long time, and he was large. The stretch would have been painful if he hadn't been so patient. He eased in a little, drawing out, and then teased her with a little more, over and over, until she was mewling with need. She was beyond turned on, and then he slipped his hand between their bodies and pressed his thumb right where she needed it.

Too much.

Not enough.

She relaxed and tensed at the same time, and he thrust all the way into her.

Crying out, she grabbed him and held on.

"More?" he asked in a low rasp.

"You have to ask?" She wrapped her legs around his waist and pushed up against him.

"If we aren't careful, we'll fall," he warned.

"Then fall." She tilted over so they toppled off the couch.

He twisted so she landed on top of him, then rolled to be back on top. "This is better. More room."

He made use of the space, spreading out over her, rolling around with her.

A sweaty tangle of limbs, she lost all sense of where she ended and he started. The intensity rose, climbing higher with each caress—each hot kiss—until she thought she was going to burst.

And then she did. She cried out, head spinning, seeing stars, hearing him moan and stiffen a moment later.

Une grande passion, her grandmother would have

called it. Eyes closed, Gwen tried to catch her breath. She didn't expect a great passion ever, much less one with Rick. She smiled. She liked it. A lot.

"That's a happy smile," he murmured, easing to one side.

"Don't let it go to your head."

"I'm in no danger of that with you." He traced her lips with his finger. "Besides, I'm fairly pleased too."

She opened her eyes. "Fairly?"

"Maybe more than fairly." He kissed her. "I just didn't want it to go to your head either."

Chapter Nine

"THAT'S NOT ACCEPTABLE, Desmond," Elizabeth said into the receiver, slamming her mug on the counter so hard that Camille was surprised it didn't shatter. "Give me a different answer."

Camille sipped her tea, trying to tap into the calmness the teabag wrapper had promised. She should be used to this. Her mornings had been the same all her life: having oatmeal at the kitchen table while her mother yelled at people on the phone to force them into interviews.

At least she had dinner with Dylan to look forward to. He'd had to fly to New York to meet with his agent and editor, but they were having dinner when he got back.

It was just a friendly dinner, she told herself, not want to blow it out of proportion.

But she couldn't help it—she grinned every time

Kate Perry

she thought of it.

"If you want this in the *New York Times*, you'll have to pick a date already," her mother yelled. "Do you think I just slap my work together? It takes time to craft an outstanding interview."

Camille's grin faded in the wake of her mother's unpleasantness. She didn't get it. Weren't you supposed to attract flies with honey? But this confrontational style worked for her mother. Even weirder, everyone spoke highly of her.

Of course, that may have been because they were kissing up to her. Elizabeth Bernard was a journalistic wunderkind.

If someone had told her that at twenty-eight Camille would still be living at home under her mother's thumb, listening to Elizabeth's abuse, she'd have jumped off the Golden Gate Bridge. She hated being there, for more reasons than she could name. She stirred her oatmeal. It'd congealed into an unappetizing grayish-brown mass.

Elizabeth tossed the phone aside. "Well, *that* wasn't helpful in the least."

She watched the phone skitter across the counter. It was amazing her mother didn't break them more often. Picking up her bowl and cup, Camille rinsed and placed them in the dishwasher. "See you later."

"Are you going to work?" Elizabeth leaned against the counter and pulled out a cigarette.

She hated when her mother lit up around her. "I wish you'd stop that."

"If wishes were horses..." Elizabeth lit the tip and took a deep drag, blowing the smoke out behind her. "What are you working on these days? A piece on salt water taffy?"

Camille heard the derision in Elizabeth's voice and felt rebellion rise up her gorge. She was in no space to pick a fight with her mother today. The last thing she needed was to be in a worse mood. She reached behind her mother and opened the window. "I have an interview."

"So do I. In fact, I'm due to call the attorney general in ten minutes." She looked at her wrist as though there was a watch there, even though she never wore one. "Who are you interviewing, Camille?"

A gourd artist. Just thinking it made her stomach sour. "A local artist."

"How quaint." Her mother smiled insincerely.

It was a special talent Elizabeth had, making her

feel like the perpetual loser.

"Would you like me to talk to your editor, Camille?" Her mother flicked ashes into the sink. "I can have him give you better assignments."

"*No.*" She shuddered to think of her mother storming into Mac's office. "I can handle it. Actually, this assignment is pretty juicy," she lied.

"Are you sure? After all, Reginald Waters and I are great friends."

This was where her mother reminded her that the only reason she was working for the newspaper was because she was "great friends" with the man who owned the publication. "I'm sure, but thank you," she forced herself to say.

Her mother eyed her as she puffed elegantly on her cigarette. "You know why I named you Camille."

Not this again. She shrank on the inside. "Yes, I know."

"I named you after a dear friend and great feminist. The original Camille wouldn't have stood for being patted on the head and sent to a corner. She'd have stood up for what she wanted and taken it."

That was the thing about being a copy of the original—the copy was always a blurry version of the original. "I'll keep that in mind."

"Please do, Camille," she said, stubbing out the cigarette on a dirty plate.

The phone rang, and she sighed in relief as her mother reached for it. "Darling," her mother effused into the receiver, a genuine smile lighting her face. "How delightful to hear from you."

Camille edged out of the kitchen while her mother was distracted. Grabbing her bag, she walked down five blocks to catch the 24. It wasn't the most direct way to get to Laurel Heights, but there wasn't any better option, other than taking a cab. On her salary, taking a taxi was a rare splurge.

She hadn't exactly told her mom the truth when she'd said she had an interview with the gourd artist. She'd tried calling the woman — Gwendolyn Pierce, the fact sheet said — but there'd been no answer. Camille figured she'd just go to the artist's shop, ask a couple questions, and get it over with.

Hopping off the bus at Sacramento Street, she strolled the rest of the way to the gourd shop — slowly, because her heels were already cutting into her feet.

Laurel Heights was a completely different world

from upper Hayes Valley, where she lived with Elizabeth. Her mother had bought the house when that area was the projects — it grew into being fashionable, although it wasn't nearly as high-end as Laurel Heights.

It was eleven in the morning. As she walked down Sacramento Street, she noted the women pushing strollers and carrying Louis Vuitton bags that cost more than she made in a month.

Camille envied them — not for their things but because they looked satisfied. She didn't belong there. She wasn't successful. She didn't have a Mercedes. She didn't lunch. Frankly, she didn't have any girlfriends to lunch with. She only had Dylan, and he wasn't really hers either.

Sometimes, late at night when she was alone, she wanted him to be.

But that wasn't going to happen. Sure, there'd been a split-second when they'd met that she'd had a crush on him, but she'd gotten over it quickly.

For the most part.

Lost in thought, she almost passed the storefront, but the colorful sign caught her attention. She stopped abruptly and peeked in the window.

Black velvet draped the whole case, and a short screen provided the background. The gourds had intricate Asian designs carved and painted on them — koi, dragons, nature — in vivid colors. The effect was rich and exotic.

It shocked her.

Inside Outta My Gourd, there was more art, similar to what was in the window and also completely different. All of it was amazing. She'd expected gourd art to be kitschy and ludicrous. Craftsy — on par with a velvet Elvis.

She picked up a clever gourd that was actually an earring keeper. The finish was satiny smooth, and the peacock detailing on the surface was intricate. She held it up to get a closer look.

"That's one of my favorites," a chipper voice said from behind her.

Camille turned around, startled.

A woman bounced out from behind. She was a blaze of color — streaky long red curls, pink tunic, orange leggings, and red kitten heels. She dressed like a bohemian artist, but the vague, dreamy look most of the artists had — at least the ones she'd met through her mother — was absent. This woman looked alert.

And happy, like she was pleased with her place in the world.

Camille felt a niggle of jealousy at that.

The woman walked toward her, a warm impish smile on her lips. "I was afraid of peacocks when I was a child. It's funny that I'd be so fascinated with them now. Go figure."

"Yes." She set the jewelry box down. "Are you Gwendolyn Pierce?"

The woman went from happy to wary. "Yes. I own this shop."

"My name is Camille Bernard." She took out a business card and held it out. "I'm with the *San Francisco Daily*. I left a message for you. I'm covering the new art exhibit at the de Young, and Jennifer Brady, the curator at the museum, told me you were part of the show. I wanted to ask you a couple questions for an article I'm writing."

Ms. Pierce stared at the card and then looked Camille in the eye. All of her previous welcome was replaced by cool politeness. "This isn't a good time."

Camille looked around. No one was there. What better time could there be? Elizabeth would have pointed that out and insisted on a one-on-one.

So would she. She pulled out her little notebook and forged ahead. "When are gourds in season? And what happens if there's a gourd shortage?"

"Shortage?"

"Like if a plague takes out the gourd crop for a year. Who gets the remaining gourds?"

"If the gourd crop was destroyed, wouldn't that mean no one would get any?"

"I guess so." Camille glanced at her next question. "Have you ever considered what you'd do if you lost a hand? Or if you went blind?"

Ms. Pierce gaped at her, for some reason. "*That's* what you're curious about?"

"They're the sorts of questions people really want to have answers to." Her mother always said the hard questions were the ones that needed to be asked.

"You don't think people want to know what inspires me? Or where I get my ideas?"

Camille made a face. "Those seem boring."

The artist shook her head. "Why don't I just say that I'm honored to be part of the exhibit and leave it at that? I'm sure that's all you need."

"I have more questions, though." She closed her notebook, frustrated. Why was this interview such a big deal? "Fine. I can come back. When's a good time?"

Ms. Pierce looked like she wanted to say never.

Just then the door tinkled open and a woman walked in. She was tall with long blond hair, wearing skin-tight yoga pants that hugged her lanky curves.

Gwendolyn turned to the woman and smiled. If Camille wasn't mistaken, there was a measure of relief to the smile. "Welcome to Outta My Gourd. Can I help you find anything today?"

The woman blinked and then slowly nodded. "Um. Yes. I guess I'm looking for a gourd."

"You came to the right place," Gwendolyn said happily. She faced Camille. "Thank you for stopping by, and good luck with your article."

Knowing she'd been dismissed, Camille murmured something appropriate and left the store, feeling defeated. How was she going to become a great journalist if not even a gourd artist would speak to her?

Albeit, the woman was truly a master at her craft. Camille wouldn't have been surprised if Ms. Pierce won the spot in the de Young's permanent collection. She deserved it.

It didn't explain why she shied away from an interview though. Even beekeepers liked the free publicity. That rug weaver Camille had to interview couldn't wait to tell her his whole life story.

Why didn't Gwendolyn Pierce want to talk?

Did Gwendolyn Pierce have a sweatshop in the back? Or—Camille gasped—an army of illegal Chinese workers who'd been sold to her to produce gourds!

Or maybe she had a dead body back there, chilling on ice.

Walking down the street, Camille glanced over her shoulder at the store. Outta My Gourd. Definitely, yes.

Gwen heaved a sigh of relief the moment the door closed behind the reporter. She'd always had an aversion to reporters, but especially since she'd run away. And Camille Bernard had a hungry look in her eyes, like she'd chew off her own leg and sell it for a good story.

"So..." Lola leaned against a display case and crossed her legs at the ankles. "Apparently I'm desperate to buy a gourd."

"You are, and good thing you realized it when you did." Gwen grinned. "Thanks for playing along."

"Mind telling me why we were pretending?"

"That was a reporter."

Lola perked up. "I love reporters."

Gwen made a face. "You do?"

"Yeah, because it means free marketing." She shrugged unapologetically. "On an author's budget, you take whatever marketing you can get, especially free marketing."

Gwen knew for a fact that Lola wasn't a starving writer like she pretended. In fact, after Lola had moved in upstairs and introduced herself, Gwen had looked up the woman's books. Lola was a romance author, with a dozen books to her name. Her latest book had been at the top of the New York Times bestseller list for weeks.

"I'd think free publicity would please you too," Lola said.

"I'm a private person." To change the subject before Lola and her inquisitive nature got too nosy, she asked, "So what brings you down here?"

"Oh, right. I wanted to invite you over for dinner."

"Pizza and champagne?" Gwen asked hopefully.

"Definitely. And I just received the latest teen dance movie from Netflix."

"Is it god-awful?"

"It got the worst reviews I've ever seen," Lola replied gleefully.

"Super." If Lola hadn't moved in upstairs Gwen would never have been introduced to the delights of dance movies with no plot. Her favorite was Step Up 2. She knew most of the dance sequences by heart.

Lola stood to her full height, which was tall. "What time are you closing?"

The door to the store opened right as Gwen started to answer. She stiffened, thinking the reporter was back.

But she wasn't. It was Rick Clancy who walked into her store.

Gwen started to smile, happy to see him, but then she remembered she was annoyed. He hadn't contacted in days, since that night they'd—what? Had sex? It'd been more than sex. Made love? That was overreaching.

Lola arched her brow, her hand going to her throat as she stared at him. Gwen couldn't blame her—Rick looked particularly delicious this afternoon in jeans and his leather jacket.

And he only had eyes for her, which both made her both worried and pleased. Pleased because Lola was a voluptuous blonde with legs that never ended. Fantasy Time Barbie, she called herself. But Rick didn't seem to notice her.

And this worried Gwen because it was an *awful* idea having his attention focused too closely on her. Even with their truce, she wasn't certain if he was interested in her or in ferreting out her secrets.

So she said the logical thing: "What are you doing here?"

He stuffed his hands in his pockets, his expression souring. "I'm asking myself that too."

Lola cleared her throat—loudly.

Gwen rolled her eyes. "This is my friend, Lola. She lives upstairs and was just leaving."

Smiling brilliantly, Lola extended her hand. "Pleased to meet you, even though I don't know who you are."

"Rick Clancy." He flashed that devilish grin of his.

Gwen had no idea how Lola managed to stay

standing. If he'd looked at her that way, she'd be a puddle on the floor.

Her friend obviously didn't have that problem though, because she gave Rick a cheeky grin before turning to give Gwen a pointed look. "Let me know if you need to change our plans."

"I won't," Gwen promised.

"Right," her friend said, though her tone screamed *Liar*. She headed to the door, turning to wink at Gwen and give her a thumbs up.

Channeling Laurel, Gwen rolled her eyes. She waited until the door clicked shut before facing Rick. "Why are you here?"

He frowned. "It's cold out."

She nodded. "This is San Francisco. It's always like this in August."

"I didn't want you rollerblading home in the fog," he explained, picking up a gourd and studying it.

She barely resisted the urge to snatch her artwork out of his hands. "What does a little fog matter?"

"It's dangerous. I'll take you home."

"*No.*" She shook her head vehemently. She'd been treated like she was some sort of fragile crystal when she was a kid, and she wasn't about to revert to that.

"You aren't my keeper. Besides, I have plans."

He set the gourd back in its exact spot and faced her. "What plans?"

"None of your business. You're the one who's been absent, so don't act like I'm at fault for living my life." She turned to walk away.

He grabbed her hand as she walked by and pulled her into his body. She contemplated pushing away, but he felt good. Why spite herself?

"I've been working a lot, and I miss you," he told her, clutching the back of her shirt in his fist and holding her flush against him. "So I'll wait and take you home after whatever you have planned. Not because I don't think you can take care of yourself but because maybe I want to spend time with you."

She melted with happiness. "Do you have a fever?"

"Early dementia." He brushed back her hair, tipping her head back.

She eased more into him. Kiss me, she wanted to whisper. "I hear they have drugs to help with that these days. Or maybe you can try electroshock therapy."

"The only therapy I need is this." He lowered his mouth to hers.

At last.

Moaning, Gwen wrapped herself around him. He hummed, backing her up until she felt the counter behind her. Picking her up, he set her on the counter and stepped between her legs, kissing her as though he didn't want it to ever end. Wrapping her legs around him, she held him close. She didn't want it to end either.

"That's what I needed," he murmured against her lips.

"Why didn't you just say so?" she asked, sighing as he slipped his hands under her shirt.

"Actions work better than words with you." He ran his hands up and down her spine, kneading gently. "Cancel your plans and take me home."

Normally, she wouldn't have, but this thing with Rick wasn't normal. Frankly, Lola would nag her all night if Gwen didn't go with him. So she nodded. "But only this time."

He stepped back from her. "What can I help with?"

She hopped off the counter. "Nothing. I need to call Lola and then lock up. Sit down. It'll only take a second."

She called Lola, who replied "Duh" when Gwen

told her she was going home with Rick. Then she quickly put away the cash and receipts, aware that he watched her the entire time. She couldn't read anything other than need in his expression.

He wanted *her*.

She shivered, delicious goose bumps of anticipation. She could almost forgive him for not calling her all week.

Maybe after she made him grovel a little.

She left her rollerblades in the back, grabbed her bag, and smiled at Rick. "Ready to go?"

"Yes." He stood and followed her out of the store, a hand on her back. It may have been wishful thinking, but it felt possessive. What surprised her more was that he took her hand after she locked the door.

She stared at their hands, clasped together, as they walked to his car. It felt good. Warm. Sweet. She liked it way more than she wanted to.

"Why are you frowning?" he asked as he held open the car door for her.

"No reason."

He looked at her like he didn't believe it.

"It's just that I'd never have taken you for the hand-holding type," she explained.

"You have nice hands," was all he said as he closed the door. But after he settled into the car he took her hand again and held it the entire way to her flat.

Chapter Ten

*I*T'D BEEN A long night. Rick had been on surveillance—a typical case where the wife suspected the husband of cheating. She'd been right, of course, and Rick had photos to prove it.

Sometimes work was demoralizing. It was hard to imagine anyone ever being honest. It was hard to trust anyone, when all you saw day in and day out was the seedy side of human behavior.

He'd planned on going home after dropping off the photos to his client and sleeping the morning away. He *had* gone home, only he was haunted by the look on the wife's face as he handed over duplicates of the photos. What really wrecked him, though, were the sad looks on her little kids' faces as they clung to her pants, sensing something was wrong with their mom but not knowing that their world was about to change forever.

Sometimes his job sucked.

He'd gone home and tried to lie down, but sleep had been elusive, so he got up, had a cup of coffee, and did the only thing he could thing of: he drove to Gwen's shop.

Why? He shook his head as he looked for parking a couple blocks away from her store. He was down on people and their inability to be honest, and yet he was choosing to seek comfort with the one person in his life he trusted least.

That was screwed up.

Parking, he went directly to her store. Gwen and the woman she was talking to stopped and stared at him. He'd seen the blonde with Gwen before—they were obviously friends. The blonde was his type, but he wasn't interested in her in the least. His body didn't react to her—not even a glimmer of a spark.

But he looked at Gwen and his entire body became alive. He walked straight to her, lifted her pointy little chin, and laid one on her.

There was nothing sweet about the kiss. It was hot and carnal and wiped the entire night and morning from his mind.

Someone cleared her throat. It took him a moment

to realize it was the other woman. He lifted his head and frowned at her.

The woman looked very amused. She winked at him and then turned to Gwen. "I'm going to leave before he escorts me off the premises. See you tomorrow?"

Gwen nodded. "Yes. Thanks again."

"Anytime." The woman winked at him and sashayed out.

He followed her, only to lock the door behind her and turn the sign to *Closed*.

"What are you doing?"

"Insuring our privacy." He walked back toward her. "Is that okay?"

"Do I have a choice in the matter?"

"Yes."

She pursed her lips in thought. "Are you going to kiss me like that again?"

"Definitely."

"Then I'm okay with it." She walked up to him, grabbed his shirt, and yanked his mouth down to hers.

The contact was everything he wanted—everything he needed. He found himself relaxing even as he tensed. She raked her fingers in his hair and he groaned with pleasure.

"The back," she muttered against his mouth.

He didn't need to be told twice. Hoisting her up, he carried her down the hall she pointed, to a room in the back.

There was a long table with all sorts of tools and little pots. Instinctively, he knew it was sacred grounds, so he set her down on a spot by the sink that was clear of any impediments.

She grabbed his head and kissed him like her life depended on it, her legs clasping tightly around his hips, pulling him close.

There were no words, only actions. He pushed down her leggings, thrilling when he found her bare beneath it. He felt her hands undo his jeans and take him out. His head fell back involuntarily the shock of her touch was so instant and electrifying.

He reached into his pocket for a condom. "I can't wait."

"Good." She rubbed herself on him, as though he were a toy there for her pleasure.

"That's not helping," he said as he fumbled with the wrapper.

"It's helping me."

He managed to ease away enough to slip the rubber on his hard-on and slowly thrust into her.

They both moaned.

Perfect. He gripped her hips, wanting to stop the moment and feel it just as badly as he wanted to push into her and take her.

She set their course when she began to rotate her hips against him. "If you're going to burst into my store and disrupt my day, you should at least perform."

"Are you taunting me?"

"I hope so."

He stopped and smiled down at her. "Thank you."

She frowned. "A little premature, aren't you? You haven't gotten there yet."

"Are you saying I should get to it?"

"That's exactly what I'm saying."

He thrust into her, over and over, so there was no room for words or commands. There were only feelings, and those feelings were *good*.

He snaked his hand under her blouse and found her naked breast—*oh god*—and taut nipple. She cried out when he touched her, and because he wanted to here her cry out again, he slipped a hand between them and touched her again, this time where it counted.

Her fingers clawed into him and her head fell back. "*Mon Dieu*," she shrieked, right before he felt her tighten around him.

He felt her climax and fell in line behind her, unable to hold out. Clutching her so she couldn't wiggle off him, he thrust one more time and followed her into oblivion. They slumped against the wall behind them, panting, his forehead pressed against hers.

She was the first one to speak. "I'm glad you stopped by."

He chuckled breathlessly. "So am I."

"This was good."

"Yes, it was."

Then she said, "Do you want to talk about what's bothering you?"

He lifted his head so he could look at her. "You could tell?"

She nodded. "But I think you feel better now."

"I do." He frowned.

A look of sadness lined her lovely face. "It bothers you, that I can help."

"It bothers me that I don't really know you." He remembered how she'd exclaimed in French during sex. "Like you've never told me you speak French."

He watched her retract, distancing herself from him, even though she didn't move a muscle. "A lot of people speak French," she said carefully.

"But not so fluently that they cry out in it as they come."

She really did pull away this time. "I thought we had a détente about you investigating me."

He wanted to draw her back to his chest and keep her there, but the distance between them was suddenly vast. "I'm not investigating, I'm making an observation."

She sat up, grabbing her shirt from the floor next to them and holding it to her chest. "Maybe this wasn't a good idea."

"It was an excellent idea." He sat up, too. He noticed the way her eyes ate up his nakedness. Good — because he wasn't even close to being done with her.

"I don't know. You obviously still want to discover my *secrets*" — she made air quotes — "and I still don't like you."

She didn't like him? He narrowed his gaze. "You

seemed to like me well enough a minute ago."

"I lust for you, but like is a different story." She reached for her pants.

Grabbing them from her, he tossed them aside and crawled over her.

"What are you doing?" she asked as she lay back down under him.

"Showing you that you like me more than you think." Hands on either side of her head, he dropped a kiss at the corner of her mouth.

"Why is it so important that I like you?" she asked, her eyes wide and fathomless. "This is just sex."

He didn't know why, and this wasn't "just sex." When he touched her, the world exploded, and that wasn't a normal thing. "My ego can't take it," he joked.

Gwen snorted, but she made no move to get away. "And you say *I'm* nutty."

"You like me." He kissed her again, on her jaw. And then on the spot at her neck that made her squirm in pleasure.

She melted under him. When she spoke, her voice was full of desire. "You'll have to do better than that to convince me."

"I can do that." He slid his hand over her subtle curves, to the core of her.

Fingernails biting into his shoulders, she moaned as her legs fell open. "You have a compelling argument."

He kissed his way down her body. "Hold on, Princess. It's about to get a whole lot more compelling."

Chapter Eleven

G WEN STOOD IN the workshop at the back of her store and studied the gourds she'd finished for the exhibit at the de Young. She was always concerned about quality, but this time she'd been especially discerning selecting the right gourds. She'd taken more time and care in creating them, longer than she normally did. She'd carefully gutted, dried, painted, and cured them.

The end result was better than she'd imagined. They were stunning, and she was highly critical of her own work.

Instead of making them glisten with shellac, she'd opted for something darker and more shadowed. She'd painted the entwined lovers in passionate embraces wrapped around the gourds.

She had Rick to thank for it. Seeing him the past couple months had opened her eyes to a new, sensual world.

Two months. She shook her head, unable to believe it. *Seeing* was the accurate word, too; *relationship* would have been overstating things. They got together for drive-by sex. Excellent drive-by sex.

Gwen told herself she was okay with it. Most of the time she believed herself.

She boxed the gourds for the museum and then, feeling restless, headed to Grounds for Thought to see Eve. When she walked into the store, Eve's barista Maggie welcomed her from behind the counter.

"Eve's at Romantic Notions," Maggie said before Gwen could ask. "She's preparing for a hot date with Treat. Although a pajama date with Treat would be hot."

"Tell me about it." Although she'd never been bowled over by Treat the way all other women were. She saw his bad boy appeal, and he *did* have a fine posterior, but he wasn't as hot as Rick. The first time she'd met Rick, his pheromones had made her blather like an idiot. Then he insulted her and she got over her tongue-tied-ness.

She smiled fondly. They still played annoyed with each other sometimes. It was fun sparring with him.

Getting a chocolate chip Madeleine for the road,

Gwen said goodbye to Maggie and headed to Olivia's lingerie store.

When she stepped into Romantic Notions, like always, she felt like she'd walked into her best friend's bedroom. Dressers with open drawers, colorful waterfalls of silk spilling out of them. Frothy piles of lace on whitewashed tables, soft drapery, and velvet chairs with pillows. It was brilliant, the way the store pulled a customer in, wrapped her in silk and warmth, and dared her to embrace her sensuality.

Olivia looked up from the rack she was sorting through. "Hey. This is a surprise."

"Maggie said Eve was over here, and I needed a break so I thought I'd come visit."

Eve's voice sounded from the fitting room. "You came just in time."

Olivia grinned. "I have this new set that was perfect for Eve."

Eve poked her head out from the velvet curtain. "She means it's perfect for Treat. A good saleswoman knows who the real customer is."

"So how is it?"

"It makes me look like I have boobs. Treat is going to love this, both on and taking it off." Winking,

Kate Perry

Eve ducked back into the dressing room.

Gwen looked down at her chest. She never wore anything beyond a camisole, and Rick seemed to enjoy finding her bare underneath. Would he enjoy finding a surprise underneath?

She turned to Olivia. "Do you have anything that might look good on me?"

Olivia blinked in surprise but recovered quickly. "I have the perfect thing. Hold on."

As Olivia went to fetch it, Gwen ambled over to a table that held a black corset thing that might have doubled as a torture device. Frowning, she picked it up and inspected it from all angles. Women willingly wore things like this? The price of pleasing a lover, she supposed.

Olivia came back holding out a bright piece of fluff in her hand. "Try this on, but I'm pretty sure it'll fit."

"How about this?" She held up the black corset.

"No, that's so wrong for you." Olivia wrinkled her nose. "You like that?"

She shrugged. "I'm a blank canvas when it comes to lingerie."

"Well, black's not on your palette." She handed over the lacy things in her hands. "Try these on. They're much more suited to you."

"Trust her, Gwen," Eve said as she emerged clothed from the dressing room. "She knows her stuff."

They were, she realized a couple minutes later in the dressing room. They were perfect. She looked at herself from all angles in the full-length mirror. A bright orange, the set made her skin look creamy and brought out the glints of copper she'd added to her hair a couple weeks before.

Even better, it was amazingly comfortable—not at all pokey or itchy like she remembered underwear to be. The cups were soft and without underwire, cut low. The thin straps looked delicate and almost in-substantial. The panties were no less invasive, wispy and delicate, alluring in their partial coverage.

And she looked *sexy*. She could see the darkened area of her nipple through the lace and somehow that made it look more alluring than if she was nude.

She tried to imagine Rick's reaction when he saw it. He'd like it. A lot.

Getting dressed, she stepped out of the dressing room to find both Olivia and Eve waiting, expectant

looks on their faces. She smiled and held it out. "I'll take it."

Eve grinned. "Want to tell us what his name is?"

She felt her face flush. "What makes you think a man is involved?"

"Because you don't like lingerie," Olivia said as she took the lingerie.

"I like lingerie." At their disbelieving looks, she added, "In theory."

Olivia began wrapping it in tissue paper. "Is it Rick?"

If her face was burning before, it was completely in flames now. She put her hands to her cheeks. "Is it that obvious?"

"Yes." Olivia grinned. "But it was obvious from the first time you guys met."

"You acted like first graders with a crush," Eve said with an amused smile. "He all but pulled on your pigtails."

"It's not anything serious," she said quickly, so they wouldn't get the wrong impression. "We're just..."

"Playing?" Olivia offered with a sly grin.

"Yes." She frowned. "It's weird."

Eve leaned against the counter next to her. "Why? Because he wants you? You're pretty and smart. The only reason you don't have men all over you is because you have a wall around you."

"Rick obviously had the equipment to scale it, though," Olivia said with a wink, handing her the little bag.

She didn't mention that he'd scaled it many times in the past few weeks. In fact, she hoped he'd climb again tonight.

Things had shifted between them. He hadn't said it in uncertain terms, but she thought he trusted her a little more now. Not completely, but she told herself that wasn't important. What *was* important was that it didn't appear as though he was investigating her. She knew they had a deal, but she hadn't thought he'd hold up his end. He was too curious a person.

Even if he were still investigating, if he were going to discover anything, he would have by now. He was too good not to. And if he hadn't uncovered anything yet, it meant that she'd covered her tracks well enough to be protected.

Was she deluding herself into a false sense of security?

Did it matter? They couldn't last—not without her telling him about her past, and she couldn't do that. She couldn't tell anyone.

"What's wrong?" Olivia asked, ever astute.

"Nothing." She smiled to cover her emotions, the way her mother had taught when she was a child. "What do I owe you?"

"It's a gift." Her friend held her hand up. "Don't protest. Think of me like a drug dealer. I have to get you hooked so you come back for more product."

"Even if she doesn't get hooked, *Rick* definitely will," Eve said with a sly grin.

"I hope so." She stayed to talk a few more minutes, but her mind was on Rick and the fact that her nights with him were numbered.

Rick drove them to Gwendolyn's, anticipating getting her home and naked. The other part of him was very happy sitting quietly with her, just holding her hand.

He was clearly losing it.

Of course he was losing it. He shook his head, thinking about how distracted he'd been during the day. He'd been putting together a background check for a client and all he'd been able to think about was her lush lips and her springy hair tickling his nose as they cuddled.

As if sensing his need for diversion, she asked with that caustic edge that made him want to both spank and kiss her, "How was your day, honey?"

He glanced at her. "Long."

"And hard?" she asked with a smirk.

"You wish."

"I *know*," she murmured with a flush. She cleared her throat. "You didn't tell me about your day."

"It was the usual."

"Peeking into women's bedroom's?"

There was only one woman's bedroom he was interested in, and he fully planned on being completely inside it, not looking in from the outside. "One time, I caught a wife I was surveilling having an affair with the nanny."

"That must have made your day."

"My month."

She pursed her lips. "Is *surveilling* really a verb?"

"It should be." He pulled into a parking spot a block from her apartment and they exited the vehicle.

She took his hand again. "Come on."

"Where?" he asked when she walked away from her street.

"I'd planned on going swimming."

He remembered her in that tiny yellow bikini and went semi-hard on the spot. "I don't have a swimming suit."

"Do you need one?"

He almost groaned out loud, thinking about being in the water, with her naked in his arms. His fingers itched to touch her all over, to plunder her.

As strong as that incentive was, he paused outside the gate, watching her scramble easily over the top. She pressed her face against the bars, grinning like a devious child, her eyes sparkling with the adventure. "What are you waiting for?"

"The Rottweiler's and uniformed officers."

She rolled her eyes. "I told you, Candace lets me use her pool whenever I want. I just can't find the key."

"Plus, it's more fun to scale the wall, right?" he said, hoisting himself up.

She grinned at him and skipped around back.

He filed the name Candace away, along with the house number. It was easy enough to check out who lived there. Somehow he believed Gwendolyn was telling the truth.

A sure sign he was losing it if there ever was one.

He rounded the back in time to see her shrug out of her jacket and toe off her shoes. Her back to him, she took her top off and dropped it on the pile before taking her pants and socks off, too. Then she turned around.

The sight took his breath away.

She stood before him in skimpy bright orange underwear that covered and revealed both at the same time. There was just enough light from the pool so that he didn't have to leave anything to his imagination. Through the lace, he could see the shadow of her nipples and the trim arrow of hair that pointed the way to heaven.

He took a step forward.

She smiled at him, a playful, seductive smile that made his groin tighten. "What are you waiting for?"

She turned again, giving him a delicious view of taut asscheeks before diving gracefully into the pool.

He stood, dumbfounded, watching her glide through the water like a water nymph. Shaking off the sexual stupor, he quickly stripped down to his boxers and jumped in too.

He came up to find her laughing and wiping the water drops from his splash from her eyes. He swam over to her, wrapping her in his arms.

She hooked her legs around his waist and let him support her in the water.

Closing her eyes, she tipped her head backwards, a smile lifting her lips. Her neck was arched, a long graceful column in the shimmery light. Under the surface, her orange underwear taunted him. He slipped a finger under its delicate strap and tugged.

With a laugh, she was suddenly out of his arms and undulating away from him.

He chased her, less gracefully. He was a strong swimmer, but he wasn't going to win any awards for form. Gwen, on the other hand, had great form *and* she was an excellent swimmer. Given his reach, he thought he'd have caught her right away, but she evaded him, her delighted laughter taunting him.

It made him smile too.

After playing for a while, she let him catch her. They wrestled in the water before they both agreed they were tired and floated side-by-side, fingers touching.

"You swim like a dolphin," he commented.

"I love the water." Eyes closed, she smiled nostalgically. "I used to swim all the time growing up. It was one of the only places that felt peaceful."

"Did you have another peaceful place?"

If he hadn't been paying such close attention, he wouldn't have noticed the slight hesitation she had before she said, "With my grandmother."

"Does she live close by?"

"No." Gwen let herself drop to tread the water. "It's a nice night."

He smiled wryly. "I get it. I won't ask about her."

She stared up at the sky, obviously thinking. Then she lowered her big eyes to him, open and guileless. "No, I think I'd like to talk about her. I miss her. She was my favorite person, my best friend."

"You talk about her like she's gone."

Her smile was sad. "She lives far away."

He nodded. "When was the last time you saw her?"

"Too long ago." She sighed. "My grandmother is the one who taught me to swim. Actually, she taught me everything useful."

"Including painting?"

"No, Bob Ross taught me that."

"Bob Ross? The dude with the afro?"

She laughed. "I saw him on TV once, calmly painting happy trees, and I wanted to try it. So I bought some paint and a set of his DVDs and started to paint."

"So Bob Ross is the reason you do gourds."

"No, Phyllis Neumann is the reason I do gourds." She grinned. "I met Phyllis in Taos, New Mexico. I ended up staying with her for a few months and apprenticing, basically."

"I didn't know you lived in New Mexico."

"Why would you? I never told you." She looked up at the sky. "I've lived in a lot of places."

He wanted to ask about that, but suddenly she was in his arms. "Tell me about your family," she said.

Holding her loosely, he smiled as he thought about his mom and dad. "They live in Boston. My dad's retired, which means my mom is, too. She used to run the office and do the accounting. I think she's trying to convince him to take up some hobby to get him out of her hair."

Gwen grinned. "I hear bird watching is popular."

"In Boston?"

"You're right." She nodded. "They probably

don't have birds in Boston."

He chuckled.

With a smile that was sad at the edges, she said, "It sounds like you're close to them."

"Yes. They hate that I live out here, especially my dad, but they love to come visit."

She nodded, looking like she was thousands of miles away.

Not liking the mental distance between them, he kissed her. Then because he liked it, he kissed her again.

She hummed, running her fingers in his hair. "You never said anything about my underwear."

"That's because I nearly swallowed my tongue." He nuzzled the edge of her jaw. "I thought you didn't wear underwear."

"Sometimes you have to try new things."

"There's a new thing I'd like to try," he said as he floated them to the edge of the pool.

Understanding brightened her gaze and she looked around. "Here?"

"You're the one who breaks in and goes skinny dipping." He pressed her against the side, bracketing her with his arms.

"I don't break in, and I always wear a swimsuit."

He arched his brow.

"Well, most of the time."

He thought about her gliding through the water naked and felt himself go from interested to fully aroused. "Take the underwear off, Gwendolyn."

Her eyes widened. He expected her to argue, but she bit her lip and wiggled out of the panties, tossing them over her shoulder. As she lifted the bra over her head, her breasts popped above the surface, rosy and taut.

He reached around her, holding her up, and sucked one into his mouth. He registered her gasp. Good—she liked it. But he liked it too, and even if she didn't he didn't think he'd stop. It was plump, like a raspberry, and just as sweet.

She arched closer to him, rubbing herself against his erection. "Take yours off too," she whispered, her voice huskier with need.

He calculated how far away his pants (which held the condoms) were and decided it was too far. He shook his head. "Later."

"But—"

Before she could do anything, he turned her

around and slid his fingers into her heat.

They both gasped.

He anchored her against him with a hand on her chest. As he teased her nipples, one by one, he stroked her between her legs.

She moaned, dropping her head on his shoulder. "That's good."

He had to agree, especially the way she hummer and moaned, rocking against his touch. He wished he had a condom at hand — he'd have given anything to take her now.

She moaned again.

"That's it." He hauled her out of the pool. For a moment, he contemplated taking her on the ground, right there, but he saw the goose bumps on her skin and tossed her clothes at her. "Get dressed."

"I'm wet."

He grinned. "I know."

She grinned too. "I have a better idea."

"What?"

"Race you home." She took off, clutching her clothes to her naked form.

"Gwendolyn!" he called after her, but all that was left of her was the echo of her laughter. He gathered his things and took off after her, cursing and laughing simultaneously. She had that effect on him.

He shook his head as he ran down the street, chasing her pale delicious ass. At least she lived close—they'd be inside before anyone could call the cops on them for streaking.

Chapter Twelve

CAMILLE SCURRIED INTO Absinthe, hating that she was twenty minutes late but knowing Dylan would wait patiently for her.

He was, at the bar, nursing a glass of wine and reading.

"Sorry," Camille said as she hopped onto the barstool next to him. "I had to do some last minute editing on the article I wrote on the underground *foie gras* scene since it's been outlawed."

He closed the book and turned to her. "Cutting edge stuff."

"It is if you're a duck."

He grinned, and it lit his entire face.

Warmth spread through her, that she'd been able to delight him. Happy for the first time in days, she smiled as she hung her things on the hook under the countertop. "I deal with all the pressing issues in my job."

"And you do it marvelously." He motioned to the bartender. "Your article on beekeeping was captivating, as was the one on feng shui. Had I known I'd inspire such great heights by helping you move your bed..."

She rolled her eyes. "If you thought that was good, just wait till you read the one I'm writing on a gourd artist."

The bartender came over and Dylan ordered her a glass of white wine. Then he angled himself to face her. "I never knew one could be such a thing as a gourd artist."

"Neither did I." She leaned in conspiratorially. "I think the whole store is a front."

"For what?"

"A prostitution ring," she said off the top of her head.

"Heavy." Amusement lit Dylan's gaze as he leaned his chin on his palm.

"It's either that or money laundering. The store is in Laurel Heights. How else would she afford her rent?" Nodding thanks at the bartender, she tried the wine. Light, crisp, and delicious. But Dylan always knew which wines would suit her palate.

"Maybe she's actually selling gourds," Dylan suggested.

She arched her brow. "You think there's a big market on gourds?"

He shrugged. "What was she like?"

"Colorful. Nice. Secretive." She pursed her lips. "She didn't really want to talk to me."

"Did you go dressed as an undertaker?"

Frowning, she glanced down at her suit. "I don't dress like an undertaker."

Dylan arched his brow as he took a sip of his wine.

"I look professional."

"I never said you didn't." He tugged the collar of her suit coat. "I know I'd come to you if I had to bury someone."

His hand brushed the top of her breast, and for a second she couldn't breathe. She exhaled with a rush and fanned herself. "Is it warm in here? I think it's warm."

"Take your coat off if you're warm," he said as though she were mental.

"Right." She shrugged out of her coat and hung it on the hook over her purse.

"Here." He reached out, unbuttoning the top couple buttons of her blouse. She'd had it done up to her neck, so it wasn't like she was indecently exposed, but the act of him undressing her caused her to flush deeper.

"Better?" he asked softly.

His face—his lips in particular—were so close. All she had to do was lean forward the tiniest amount and she'd be pressed to him.

And how horrifying would that be? He thought of her as his little project and she was getting it on with him in her head. She swallowed thickly and managed to squeak, "Fine."

He studied her with his all-encompassing gaze a moment longer. Then he said, "What sort of secrets do you think she had?"

Camille blinked, discombobulated. "What?"

"Your gourd artist. What sorts of secrets does she keep?"

Without thinking, she said, "She was spurned by a paperboy when she was a teenager and has been harboring a hatred for anyone tied to journalism ever since. She was planning on killing me and stuffing me in a gourd."

Dylan shook his head. "Your talents are wasted. You should be writing fiction."

Just like that, she went on guard. "I'm a journalist."

"You're a writer," he insisted. "A good writer, and a good writer can write anything he wants."

"If I'm good enough to write anything, why can't it be news? Why are you always trying to get me to change my focus?" She picked up her wine so she'd have something to do with her hand, but she didn't try to drink any, afraid she might choke.

"Because your purpose isn't telling people what's already happened." Impassioned, he turned to bracket her with his legs. "It's entertaining people with your unique point of view."

She remembered the harsh red letters her mother had scrawled on her partial manuscript and felt something in her wither all over again. "You're wrong."

"I'm not wrong," he said, his voice low with intent. "I'm an author. I recognize talent."

"Can we talk about something else?" she asked plaintively, starting to turn away.

"No, we can't." He took her by the arms so she had to face him. "Didn't you hear yourself as you were talking about this gourd artist? You took a nugget of reality about her and spun it into an intriguing character."

"I just told you what I thought about her."

"You wove her into a compelling character I want to know more about." Dylan's gaze burned with passion. "I want to know why she became a gourd artist and what inspires her. I want to know how she affords the store, and why she decided to open it in Laurel Heights. I want to know what her secrets are."

Camille blinked. "So you're saying I should investigate her?"

Dylan sighed, clearly exasperated. "Of course not. I'm telling you to *create* her. Make her into whoever you want her to be. Weave her into an adventure."

She couldn't do that, but she could find out who the real Gwendolyn Pierce was. Because Camille's usually dormant journalistic instincts told her that there was more to Gwendolyn's story than she let on.

It could even be her big break. She'd joked about money laundering, but what if...?

She had to calm down, she told herself. It was no good getting worked up for nothing. Most stories turned out to be duds.

"Aren't you going to say anything?" he asked.

She looked up at Dylan, surprised to find his face so close to hers, with his hand cupping her cheek. His thumb caressed the edge of her mouth.

Her gaze dropped to his lips. She'd always wondered what it'd be like to kiss him. She'd never been able to decide if he'd be hot and enthusiastic or slow and deliberate. If she tipped forward—just a little— she could find out.

And possibly ruin their easy friendship, making everything awkward between them.

So she leaned back. "Didn't you promise me food?"

"Not until you answer me."

She nodded. "I'll work on it."

His eyes narrowed. "You promise?"

"Yes." Just not a fictional one, she added silently.

"Good," he said. "Promise me one other thing."

"What?" She took a sip of wine.

"Go out with me again."

"For dinner?"

He smiled ruefully. "And more. If you want."

"Like for dessert?" Then she gasped as she saw the expression on his face. "Surely not *dessert*."

"Yes," he said with an amused smile. "*Dessert.*
Eventually, at least. First I just want a real date."

"*With me*?"

"Of course, you." Frowning, he touched her
cheek. "It's time, Camille."

Her heart beat a mile a minute. This was a bad
idea. She didn't have anything to offer him. She was
a loser at work. She was so much younger and wasn't
interesting like the women he usually dated. She
wiped her sweaty palms on her skirt. She should tell
him no, because it'd only mess up their friendship.

But he was *so close*, and she felt his breath on her
skin, and it made her wonder. So she said, "Okay."

"Good."

Was he going to kiss her? She leaned forward,
curious. Ready.

Wanting it.

But then the bartender returned, asking if they
wanted to order dinner. She didn't know whether to
be relieved or irritated.

She did know she needed to prove herself worthy of him, though—now more than ever. She had
his attention, but how would she hold it if she didn't
measure up to the women he was used to?

She'd go back to ask Gwendolyn Pierce more questions. If there was a compelling story to the mysterious gourd artist—and Camille believed there was—she'd be the one to break it.

Chapter Thirteen

THE PHONE RANG as Gwen was cleaning a batch of hard-skinned gourds she'd just received from her supplier. Gourd still in hand, she wiped her free one on her pants and reached to answer it. "Outta My Gourd."

There was the predictable chuckle on the other end, and then a woman said, "I'd like to speak to Gwendolyn Pierce."

"Speaking." She placed the phone in the crook of her neck so she could continue as she talked.

"I'm Jennifer Brady, the curator at the de Young Museum. We spoke a few months ago regarding the past and present exhibit. I wanted to let you know your pieces were one of the artworks selected to remain in our permanent exhibit."

Gwen dropped the gourd, screaming in a way that would have made her Gallic ancestors cringe.

Jennifer laughed. "I seem to get that reaction from everyone."

"You're the Grim Reaper in opposite." Laughing, Gwen picked up the gourd and did a little dance with it on the spot. Wait until Rick heard. She thought about their bet and laughed. It was going to be so sweet when he handed over that hundred dollars. "This is amazing."

"I have some paperwork for you to fill out, the usual contracts." There was a rustle over the line. "A release that gives your work to the museum as well as the publicity release, plus a couple other formalities. We'll courier the paperwork to you."

The pit of her stomach dropped. "Publicity release?"

"Yes, to use your name and photos. You're going to be all over, if I have anything to say about it. You're going to be the most renowned gourd artist ever. Your face and name will be splashed all over the national papers."

"No splashing!" she exclaimed. "I don't want to be splashed."

But Jennifer was so focused on her plans she didn't note Gwen's panic. "But we'll start with local news, of course, like the *San Francisco Daily*. They're doing another article on the show. I believe they've already contacted you. It's a full spread with photos of you and your artwork."

Remembering the reporter with the hungry eyes, her stomach twisted. "I'm allergic to interviews."

"We also have a member fundraiser planned, and you'll need to make a special appearance that night. It's a lot of fun. You get dressed up and schmooze and get your picture taken for the society pages."

Dread mounting, Gwen let her head thump against the wall. "I'm allergic to society, too."

Jennifer laughed. "You're funny, but then I figured with a store called Outta My Gourd you'd have to have a sense of humor. Most of the artists I deal with are quiet recluses."

"That describes me, too." She swallowed thickly. "What happens if I don't want to be part of the publicity?"

"I'm afraid publicity is part of the deal," Jennifer explained in a tone that showed her confusion. "I understand the desire for privacy, but I can guarantee you this is a good thing for both your future as an artist as well as your store."

Olivia and Eve had told her the same thing, but that was before having her picture plastered in newspapers was a reality. Thinking about her family, she shook her head. "I don't know that it is."

"Not only will you be in a featured exhibit that'll be traveling, but we'll have some of your artwork for sale in the museum store. And the publicity for your store will be invaluable. You can't buy that sort of marketing. You'll see."

"I—"

"I'll get the contracts to you ASAP," Jennifer said, overriding her. "Take your time and go over them. I'm here if you have any questions or other concerns."

"I'll definitely have concerns," she mumbled.

Jennifer congratulated her again and before she hung up, added, "I understand your hesitation, but this is going to change your life."

Was it ever.

Gwen winced as she hung up. What had she done?

Gwen burst into Grounds for Thought more forcefully than she'd intended. The door banged against the wall and bounced back into her.

"Ouch," she muttered, rubbing her arm as she walked to where Eve stood at the counter.

"That was some entrance," her friend said with a hint of amusement. "Are you okay?"

"No." She frowned. "Do you have anything stronger than tea? Like whiskey?"

"Since when do you drink whiskey? Especially at"—Eve checked her watch—"two in the afternoon?"

Since she'd sent her artwork to a famous museum and been selected to be *splashed* all over the media. She propped her elbows on the counter and dropped her head into her hands. What had she been thinking?

"Okay, Gwen, you're scaring me."

She looked up into Eve's concerned face. "You'll think I'm crazy."

"You make a living on gourd art. I already think you're crazy." She grinned. "But I love you, so your quirks are endearing. Should we go sit down so you can tell me what's up?"

"Yes." She pursed her lips in thought. "Maybe you should bring a couple madeleines with you."

Eve laughed. "Sure thing. Go sit in the window.

I'll just tell Maggie to cover for me."

True to her word, Eve came with a small plate of chocolate chip madeleines and a pot of chamomile tea. "To soothe your nerves," she said as she poured the tea.

Gwen bit into one of the cookies and hummed. "This is almost as satisfying as a shot of whiskey. At least in theory, because whiskey is disgusting."

"Are you going to tell me what's driving you to drink?" Eve leaned back and crossed her legs, bouncing her foot.

"Pretty shoes," she said, pointing to the bright violet mules her friend wore. On the top, they are two decorative buttons: one orange and one green. Eve always had cute shoes.

"Nice try in distracting me." Eve tucked her hair behind her ear, waiting patiently.

She sighed. "The de Young called me today. I won the placement in the permanent collection."

Eve exclaimed so loudly the people around them turned to look. Gwen flushed, smiled apologetically.

"That's so great," Eve enthused. "Does Olivia know? She's going to be psyched."

"I just found out. No one knows."

"No one knows what?" a very masculine voice said from over her shoulder.

Rick. Eyes narrowed, she turned to glare at him. "This is your fault."

"It's always my fault." He grabbed a nearby empty chair and sat on it backwards, resting his forearms across the back. "What did I do this time?"

"You goaded me into entering my art in the de Young's contest." If she hadn't wanted to prove him wrong about her talent, she wouldn't have entered. He also inspired the designs she created, arguably the best work she'd ever done.

But, fact of the matter: she hadn't been able to resist the lure of being recognized for her work. It'd been her own resentment of living in the shadows that had put her in this corner. She had no one to blame but herself.

Still, blaming Rick was more satisfying.

He stared at her, his expression sorry. She realized he thought she lost.

Eve must have had the same realization, because she said, "She won, Rick. They're putting her gourds in the permanent collection."

"They did?" he asked, facing her. "That's amazing."

In his expression, she saw that he was pleased for her, and it did something to her insides. The fear of discovery that'd solidified in her chest thawed a little, and she let herself enjoy the news, just a little, for the first time. "It *is* amazing, isn't it?"

"Pumpkin art often is."

She whacked his arm.

Shaking her head, Eve stood up. "I have cookies in the oven I need to check on. Do you guys need a referee, or will you behave?"

"How do you define 'behave?'" Rick asked.

Chuckling, Eve left them.

He returned his attention to her. "So what's wrong?"

"Wrong?"

"You're not gloating nearly enough. If you aren't taking the opportunity to rub this in my face, something must be wrong."

Arms crossed, she shrugged. "Maybe I'm being a gracious winner."

"And I'm Cinderella."

"If the shoe fits..."

He grinned, slow and sexy. Any worries she had about cooperating with the media or being found out took a backseat to the pleasure of seeing the pride on his face.

She cleared her throat. "Don't think I've forgotten our bet."

"Of course you haven't."

Leaning forward, she said, "I'm going to take great joy in collecting."

"Tease." He traced a finger down her arm. "We should celebrate."

Her skin tingled in the wake of his touch. "Before or after I collect?"

"Tell you what." He leaned in, close enough that she went giddy at the scent of him. "You collect first, and I'll collect second."

Swallowing thickly, she nodded. "That sounds equitable."

"It's win-win." Rick grinned. "Tonight?"

"Tonight," she promised.

Chapter Fourteen

CAMILLE SHIFTED FROM foot to foot, wincing at the pain inflicted by her pumps. The evil salesperson in Macy's had claimed were comfortable.

Comfortable if you were used to walking barefoot on broken glass. It was only ten in the morning and already her feet were done.

She leaned against Outta My Gourd's doorway. Gwendolyn Pierce had to arrive soon. Tapping the newspaper in her hand against her leg, Camille glanced at the store hours for the hundredth time in the two hours she'd been waiting. *Open from when I arrive 'til when I leave.* Who did that?

Looking up the street at the cafe a couple blocks away, she wondered if she had enough time to grab a coffee and be back before the woman arrived. But just as she started to move she saw a figure rollerblading toward her from that direction, a blaze of green, orange, and pink. It didn't take a rocket scientist to figure out it was Gwendolyn Pierce.

The bright smile on Gwendolyn's face dissolved the moment she saw Camille waiting in the doorway. The woman skated up the handicap access at the end of the block and rolled to a stop in front of the store. "This is expected yet unpleasant," she said, fishing in her pockets.

"Congratulations on getting into the de Young, Ms. Pierce." Camille smiled with extra friendliness. "It's deserved. Your artwork is surprisingly nice."

"It that supposed to be a compliment?" the woman asked as she produced a single key on a ring.

"Yes, of course." She steeled herself—she was doing this—and pushed ahead. "I'm writing an in-depth article on you, and I thought we could take care of those questions I had before."

"You're not going to relent, are you?"

"No, I'm not, Ms. Pierce," Camille said firmly.

"Then you might as well come in." She pointed a warning finger at Camille. "No pictures. And stop calling me Ms. Pierce. My name is Gwen."

"Okay." Why didn't she want pictures taken? Was she hiding from the drug cartel? Maybe she *was* into money laundering.

Her imagination spun so quickly that she didn't realize Gwendolyn had left her standing outside until the door clicked shut. Shaking out of her reverie, she walked inside.

Inside, the woman was perched on a stool, unbuckling her rollerblades. She set them behind the counter and walked to the back.

Should she follow? Camille didn't know. She was still debating when Gwen returned, carrying a tray. She'd also put shoes on, cute olive green Mary Janes that looking enviably comfortable.

The woman put the tray on the counter and pointed. "Bring that stool here and sit."

Whatever it took to get the interview. She dragged the seat over and perched on top of it, setting her purse and newspaper on the counter. "So I thought we'd start with —"

"Put this on." Gwen shoved an apron at her.

She stared at it, dumbfounded. "Are we cooking?"

"No, we're painting. I didn't want you to get anything on your suit." Pulling a stool from behind the counter, the artist perched on it and pulled two virgin gourds from the tray. "I've prepped these gourds already, meaning I've soaked, scrubbed, and sanded them before setting them to dry. "

Camille took the one she was handed and stared at it helplessly. It was long, skinny, and a little knobby on one side.

"Usually I sketch the design in pencil and then burn it in," Gwen explained, setting her own gourd in front of herself. "Sometimes I use masking tape to create patterns. But in the interest of time we're going to skip those steps and just paint."

"We are?"

"You wanted to know all about me, right? What better way to delve into the world of gourds?" the woman asked, looking way too gleeful.

She took the brush Gwen shoved into her hand but shook her head. "I can't paint."

"You don't have to know how to paint. You just do it." Gwen laid out a couple brushes and made a palette of colors for them to share. "Let the shape of the gourd inspire a design."

Turning her gourd this way and that, Camille tried to see something in it, but all she saw was a misshapen phallus. She could paint it flesh-colored, she guessed.

"I volunteer at the Purple Elephant. It's a non-profit art center for kids," Gwen said, merrily dabbing paint on her gourd. "Some of the kids come in without any knowledge of drawing or painting. I tell them it's not a matter of knowing what to do, it's allowing yourself to be free enough to see possibilities."

Camille nodded. "My squash has only one possibility that I can see, and that wouldn't be appropriate in most circles."

Gwen laughed, a soft husky sound that made Camille smile too.

The artist pointed with a brush. "What if that were a windy path? Or a stream that curves? What'd be around it?"

"Fish," Camille said without thought.

"Okay, then." Gwen arched her brow.

Not sure if she felt encouraged or challenged, Camille picked up a brush and studied her gourd. Maybe a small school of fish.

She began putting little splotches representing the fish, one by one, adding more splashes of color for variety. Some seaweed, and then a shark chasing one little fish.

Privately, she named the shark Elizabeth.

She realized too late that she should have filled the blue water in first. Cursing under her breath, she hunched over and painstakingly dabbed blue between the fishes. It wasn't elegant, but it created an interested expressionistic effect.

"Let me see," Gwen said suddenly, startling Camille. The woman inspected the gourd carefully without touching the paint. "Not bad at all, especially for someone who thinks she can't paint."

She flushed with pride, knowing it was ridiculous to feel that way but unable to help herself. "You think so?"

"Yes. I like the shark. You should have seen my first painting."

"You're just being nice."

"No, I didn't always know I wanted to be a painter. My parents wanted me to do other things that didn't suit me as much."

Camille swallowed thickly, feeling an odd kinship. "So how did you learn to paint?"

"Bob Ross."

She blinked. "The PBS guy with the afro?"

Gwendolyn laughed. "Everyone says that. Yes, I started with his happy little trees and moved on to gourds. The progression was more logical than it sounds."

"You liked gourd art so much that you opened a store?"

"Obviously." But the woman's smile was indulgent and she picked up the tray. "I'll set this to dry and then glaze it. Come back at the end of the week to collect it."

"I can have it?" Camille asked, strangely delighted. She slung her purse over her shoulder and picked up the newspaper.

"Of course. You made it." Then Gwen's smile faded slowly. Setting the tray down with a clack, she held her hand out. "Can I see your newspaper?"

"Sure." She handed it over, watching tears fill Gwen's eyes. "Are you okay?"

The woman didn't answer her, deeply engrossed in the article on the front page of the paper. Camille craned her neck to see what it was. The article on the matriarch of one of France's oldest wine families who'd passed away a few days ago.

She looked back at Gwen. Why would she be so upset?

Before she could ask, Gwen cleared her throat.

"I'm sorry. I need to go. I feel my allergies coming on."

So suddenly? Suspicious, Camille took the newspaper and headed for the door. Just as she started to open it, she remembered the interview.

Great. She mentally smacked her forehead as she turned to face the artist. "I have a few more questions. Should we set up a time for me to come back? Maybe when I pick up my gourd? I need to complete the article by the end of the week." A blatant lie—she had as long as she needed for this, but Gwendolyn didn't need to know that.

The artist shook her head. "I don't have my calendar with me."

Camille frowned. "Are you okay?"

For a moment she didn't think Gwen was going to answer, but then she said, "I'll be fine. Thanks for stopping by."

The woman escorted her out of the shop so subtly that Camille didn't realize she'd been herded out until she was standing outside.

What was that about?

Gwendolyn had seen something in the paper that'd upset her. Camille walked away from Outta

My Gourd and then poured over the newspaper.

The only thing on the open page was a couple ads for local funereal services and a long article on the matriarch of the de la Roche empire. Frowning, she skimmed through it again.

Until she got to the end. Blinking, Camille read it again, more carefully this time.

It was a standard detailed obituary, the kind that was run on celebrities and famous people. As the head of one of the biggest wine dynasties in the world, Yvette de la Roche was definitely famous.

But the last paragraph stood out: *de la Roche is survived by her two sons, a daughter-in-law, and a grandson. Her only granddaughter, Geneviève de la Roche, disappeared mysteriously fourteen years before and is presumed dead.*

Geneviève... Camille stared at the name, goose bumps rising on her skin. Still staring at it, she hurried down the street to catch the bus. She had some research to do.

Chapter Fifteen

THE SECOND CAMILLE Bernard cleared the threshold, Gwen locked the door and ran upstairs to Lola's apartment. She pounded on the door, knowing her friend tended to listen to music loudly as she worked.

But Lola opened the door immediately. "Are you okay? You're out of breath."

"I ran up the stairs." She walked in. "Can I use your laptop for a moment?"

"Of course." Closing the door, she led Gwen to the spare bedroom-slash-office. "You know, you need to break down and get a computer for the store. I can't believe you don't have one. You're the only person I know who doesn't have an email address."

The Internet was convenient and useful, but it brought people close and made the world small. She'd always needed distance and privacy. "I'll be quick," she promised as she sat at the desk.

"Take as long as you need. I was stuck with my scene anyway." Lola touched her shoulder. "Are you okay?"

Tears burned her nose, but she sniffed them back. "I think someone I knew died. I just want to check."

"Oh." Sadness filled her friend's face. "I'll leave you alone. Holler if you need anything."

Nodding, she opened a browser to Google News. At the end of the Top Stories section, there was a link that read *Yvette de la Roche, Wine Matriarch, Dies at 90*.

Clicking on it, she waiting impatiently for it to load and then skimmed through it. She gave a shuddery sigh when she found what she was looking for, that her grandmother died quietly in her sleep.

Gwen went back and read the article slower, frowning more and more with each sentence. It said how Yvette had married into the de la Roche family when she was twenty, and how she'd helped her husband turn the company from a boutique winery into a world-renowned force. It stated how she had two sons later in life, and how her husband passed away twenty-five years before her.

It had none of the real facts about her grandmother, just a flat version of some rich woman's life.

Her grandmother had been an extraordinary woman.

Gwen glared at the screen. They didn't say anything about what made Mamie Yvette so special. It didn't talk about the little terrier she'd found in the gutter and adopted, or how she adored chocolate éclairs. It didn't report that she loved to wear red even though she thought the color too vibrant for a woman her age. It didn't say that she loved to dance by the light of the moon to Frank Sinatra, or that once she drank champagne out of her dance slipper, and that she missed her husband with every waking moment.

It didn't talk about how she used to take her granddaughter on walks and tell her stories of true love and passion.

Gwen stared at the wedding photo of her grandparents. It was a copy of the one her grandmother had kept on her bed stand. When Gwen was a little girl, she used to climb on Mamie Yvette's bed, pick up the photo, and cuddle up with the picture. Back then, she loved seeing her grandmother looking like a princess. Now she saw the love in her grandparents' eyes as they looked at each other.

She scrolled past that to the next one, of her grandfather. She didn't think of him often, not the way she did of Yvette, but she remembered him to be quiet and introspective. He used to slip her caramels whenever her father wasn't looking.

Next was an official family portrait, taken sometime recently. Everyone had aged, except her mother. Her grandmother sat in the middle, with Gautier and Jacques flanking either side of her. Her brother Roger stood next to his father, and her mother hovered next to him.

Gwen was surprised by how much Roger had aged. In the picture, he looked tired and disappointed. She touched the screen, outlining his face. They'd never been close, but he'd always been kind to her despite their age difference—and the circumstances.

She looked at her mother. Like always, Janine looked perfect. Fashionable and beautiful—the ultimate trophy wife.

Her mother used to dress Gwen just like her. It was really the only reason she'd liked having a daughter, as a reflection of herself. That, and for revenge on her husband.

Her uncle Jacques looked the same as always—

dashing and handsome, with a glint in his eyes. In the dictionary, next to "international playboy" there was a picture of him.

She scrolled down some more and stalled on photos of herself.

The first one was the infamous jelly-faced picture that had won her the Grape Princess title. It used to bother her to see it, but now she thought it was cute. If she ever had kids, she wouldn't squash their spirits the way Gautier had squashed hers that day.

The next one was taken a year before she left, when she was twenty. Her hair was pulled back in a smooth chignon, and she had immaculate makeup with shiny pink-glossed lips. At her ears and neck, she had pearls, and she wore black.

She almost didn't recognize herself. She looked very much like her mother. The unhappiness radiated from her posture in the picture.

After she ran away, she swore she'd never wear black again.

The caption at the bottom read: *Called the Grape Princess as a child, Geneviève de la Roche disappeared fourteen years ago without a trace. Never declared legally dead, she stands to inherit a portion of the de la Roche wine empire.*

The article ended with one more photo of her grandmother. It looked like it was taken more recently, given the new wrinkles lining her face. She smiled politely, humor in her eyes, her hand at her lapel, touching the jeweled pin there.

Gwen gasped. It was the diamond shoe pin she'd given her grandmother one year for Christmas. Mamie Yvette had told her she'd think of her whenever she wore the pin.

Lola reentered the room and shoved a box of Kleenex in her face. "Here."

She looked up in question.

"You're crying," her friend said.

She touched her face. She hadn't realized the tears had leaked. She grabbed a couple tissues from the box and wiped her eyes and face. "Thank you."

"Want to talk about it?"

For a second she was tempted to tell Lola—to confess that her heart hurt because she'd never see her grandmother again, to admit she was the missing Grape Princess. That she'd been a pawn between her parents until she'd decided to leave. That she'd been in hiding all these years, recreating herself into someone she liked.

But she couldn't.

"Someone I knew a long time ago died," she said simply, closing the browser and clearing the cache. She didn't own a computer, but that didn't mean she couldn't use one. She had years practice covering up her tracks.

"I'm sorry to hear that." Her friend studied her. "You obviously loved whoever it was."

Tears obscured her vision, and she grabbed another couple Kleenex to press against her eyes, to stem the flow. When she felt under control, she threw away the soppy tissues.

"Thank you," she said to Lola again, standing up. On impulse, she hugged her.

Lola patted her back reassuringly. "Are you okay, really? Because you can tell me anything, and I won't repeat a word to anyone. I know we haven't known each other long, but I'm trustworthy."

"I"—Gwen shook her head as she choked up—"can't talk about it now. But maybe later."

"I'm sorry." Lola looked sad for her. "Is there anything I can do?"

Bring Mamie Yvette back, she wanted to say, so she could have *chocolat chaud* with her just one more time.

But she just shook her head and grabbed another tissue. Right then she just wanted to go home, make her grandmother's favorite tea, and look through her box of mementos.

Lola walked her to the door. "Call me, okay? So I know you're okay. Or if you need anything. I make deliveries."

Gwen hugged her again. "You're going to make me cry again."

"That's not exactly a challenge at the moment."

With a watery chuckle, she went back downstairs, collected her things, and went home to be alone with her grief.

Outta My Gourd wasn't open.

Squinting into the window, Rick tried to see if anyone was inside. In vain—all the lights were off.

Something was wrong. He could feel it in his gut.

Grabbing the doorknob, he rattled it. He didn't know why—of course it was going to be locked.

He could pick it.

He checked the time. Four in the afternoon. Gwendolyn should have been there. She hadn't been there yesterday afternoon either. He'd tried calling her but gotten her answering machine. He'd even stopped by her apartment last night, hoping to catch her sneaking out for a late-night swim.

No sign of her.

Where the hell was she? Was she avoiding him? He didn't like that thought at all.

Frowning at the door, he shoved his hands in his pockets to keep from breaking in. She wouldn't appreciate him nosing in on her business, even if she were lying hurt somewhere.

Olivia might know where Gwendolyn was. He strode down the street to his friend's lingerie store.

Olivia was on the phone when he walked in. Kissing her on the forehead, he leaned against the register and waited for her to finish.

She barely gave him a look. She jotted down some numbers, repeated what sounded like gibberish about widows and lace, and then hung up. She wrote down a couple more things before she closed her notebook and faced him. "Hello, Stranger. I'm surprised to see you walk into this store when we all know you've taken a liking to another store down the block. Or is it the lovely store owner?"

"Gwendolyn's more than lovely, but I'm not going to rise to your bait tonight."

Olivia smirked. "You're not?"

"Have you seen her?"

"Gwen?"

"No. Miss Piggy." He shook his head. "Of course, Gwen. I haven't heard from her in a couple days, and every time I've stopped by her store it's been closed."

"Wait." Olivia leaned forward, giving him her full attention. "Her store's been closed for two days?"

"At least in the afternoons. That's not her normal pattern. When she volunteers, it's later in the afternoon. She's more prone to coming in late than leaving early." Just thinking about it made him more concerned.

"You seem to know her schedule really well," Olivia said slyly.

He rolled his eyes. "Taunt me later. First help me figure out where Gwendolyn is."

"You promise I can tease you later?"

"Yes."

"And say I told you so, because I *did* tell you that you and Gwen would be good together."

"Fine. Whatever. Just help me."

Olivia frowned. "You're really worried about her."

"My gut tells me something's up."

She straightened, at attention. "Your gut's never wrong."

"No kidding."

"Okay, she hasn't opened her store in a couple days? Are you sure? That's not like her. You tried calling her cell?"

Rick leaned against the counter, arms crossed, and arched his brow.

"Okay. Silly question." She picked up the phone. "Have you been by Eve's yet?"

"No."

Nodding, she punched a button. There was a pause and then Olivia said, "Hey, Eve, it's me. Have you seen or heard from Gwen?"

Rick resisted the urge to grab the phone as he listened to Olivia's uninformative hums.

"Okay, let me know if you hear from her." Olivia hung up, her brow furrowed. "No sign of her, and Gwen is religious about her croissants."

The unease he was feeling persisted. He rapped the counter with his knuckles. "I'm going to try her apartment again."

"Okay." Olivia followed him to the door. "She probably just has a cold or something."

"Does she get sick often?"

"No." Olivia squeezed his arm. "And when you call me later to let me know that she's fine, you can also tell me how you know where she lives, because she and I have been friends for a couple years now and I still haven 't seen her place."

"You're going to give me a hard time about this, aren't you?"

"Definitely." She grinned. "Go find your woman."

It was a testament to his state of mind that he didn't argue about Gwendolyn not being his.

He made it to her Narnia in record time and found a parking spot right in front. Locking his car, he strode to the front door and buzzed the front door. When there was no answer, he buzzed it again.

And again.

And again.

He was surveying the fence to jump over it when the speaker crackled and he heard her say, "Yes?"

Her voice was listless—lackluster—completely unlike her. "Gwendolyn? Open the door."

There was a pause before she said. "Now's not a good time, Rick."

The pause told him she'd considered letting him in, and that affected him more than he'd have guessed. "Now's the perfect time. Open up and tell me what's going on."

"Go away."

"No, and if you don't cooperate, I'll get in on my own. You're the one who pointed out the futility of fences."

There was a long moment of silence, and then the door buzzed open.

She was standing in the doorway of her apartment, waiting for him with a glare. She wore a ratty sweatshirt hanging off her shoulder à la *Flashdance* with boxers that peeked from the bottom. Socks pooled at the bottom of her lean legs, and her curls looked bed-rumpled.

If it hadn't been for the dark circles under her eyes, he'd have been all over her. Instead he walked up and stood before her, wanting to touch her but instinctively knowing to wait. "What happened?"

Her eyes glistened. Tears? His chest tightened at the thought of her in distress. She looked like she'd lost her best friend.

The hopelessness on her face panicked him—he'd never imagined seeing her with anything other than that Pollyanna grin. So he did the only thing he knew how to do: he goaded her into anger.

Sniffing, he asked, "When was the last time you showered? Are you sick?"

"Sick of you." Her glare reassured him, but then it lost some of its potency with the tears that pooled in her eyes. "I told you to go away."

He shook his head, walking slowly toward her. "No chance, Princess. Not until you tell me what's wrong."

"I told you not to call me that, and the only thing wrong is that you won't leave me alone." A tear slipped down her cheek.

He knew at that moment she needed a fight more than she needed sympathy, so he crowded her in the doorway. "By the way, this hairstyle is really working for you."

She whacked his arm. "Don't touch my hair."

"Why? Do you have birds living in there?" Actually, he kind of liked her hair like that. It was the way she looked after they'd made love, tousled and rumpled by his hands.

A few more tears leaked down her face, but her gaze sparked a little with a shadow of her usual spirit. She hit him again. "You're a jerk."

If calling him a jerk was all it took to cheer her up, he'd give her synonyms. He pressed up against her and smirked. "Is that all you've got?"

She hit him again. "Only an idiot would persist where he wasn't welcome."

"Am I really not welcome, Princess?" He ran a hand over her chest, feeling the tautness of her nipple through the worn cotton. "That's not the message I'm getting."

She looked up at him, her eyes full of sadness, and said, "Fu —"

He pressed his mouth to hers and stole her words.

She didn't struggle, instead channeling her aggression into their embrace. She yanked him closer by the collar of his leather jacket and wrapped her legs around his waist. He anchored her to him with his hands under her, moving them inside and kicking the door closed.

He tasted her tears, steadily running down her face, and felt a strange combination of sadness, helplessness, and something else. He didn't know what to do to heal her obvious wound, so he did the only thing he could — he kissed her harder.

She mewled and wiggled closer as she felt his fingers slide into the leg of her boxer shorts. "Bedroom," she mumbled against his mouth.

Somehow he got them into her room, naked, and on the bed without major bodily damage. She anchored her legs on his and reached between them to grab him.

Damn it, he forgot the condom. Not wanting to stop her, he scrabbled for his pants. She held him closer, as if she thought he was trying to get away.

Never — and to assure her, he speared his free hand into her hair and ravaged her mouth, her neck, and then worked his way down to her breasts, licking the tips until she writhed under him.

She yanked him up by the hair. "Now."

"Okay." He lunged for his pants, withdrew the condom, covered himself, and drove into her.

Incredible. It'd been good the first time, but now he was beginning to know her, to know her body, and it was that much better. He knew that she'd gasp when he thumbed her nipple. A swivel of his hips and she'd arch up. And as she got closer to climax, her fingernails would bite into his asscheeks.

Like they were now.

"Please," she pled against his lips. "Please."

"Yes." He thrust, taking her again and again, triumphant that desire had revived her light and banished her sadness, at least temporarily. Then he was thoughtless as she rolled her hips over and over —

Until they both cried out.

Wave after wave rode over him, and he held her close until the only thing left to do was collapse on top of her. He listened to her trying to catch her breath, felt the rapid beat of her heart under his, and held her even closer.

She burrowed in to his shoulder. "Thank you."

"Anytime." He smiled when he felt her lips curve against his skin.

Rolling over, he gathered her to his side and caressed her hair from her face so he could see her eyes. "You want to tell me what's going on?"

She hesitated, and he didn't think she was going to tell him. But then she said, "My grandmother died."

That feeling she always seemed to spark in his

chest flared, and he held her closer. "I'm sorry," he murmured, kissing her temple.

She nodded with a little sniffle.

"I didn't know you had a grandmother." She never talked about her family.

"I'm estranged." She started to move away from him.

"Don't." Pissed that she was shutting herself off from him, he pulled her closer. He wanted to pound that wall of hers with his fists and get to her inner sanctum. He didn't delude himself in thinking he could just walk away anymore. Fact of the matter: she was a puzzle, and he'd never been able to set a puzzle aside until he'd solved it.

Only he was beginning to think it's take more than a lifetime with her, and even then he'd barely scratch the surface.

He didn't mind.

"I'm sorry you were estranged from your grandmother. You obviously love her." He paused, and then added, "And I'm sorry for your grandmother. Not seeing you must have been sad for her."

Gwen's eyes filled and she buried her head in his neck.

He soothed her back. "Tell me something about her."

Rick didn't think she was going to, but softly she began. "When I three, I fell into the pool and almost drowned. Consequently, I was scared of the water. It terrified me."

"But you're like a fish," he said.

"Because of my grandmother." She smiled sadly. "My grandmother took me by the hand, every day, and walked me to the edge of the pool. She told me stories of magical creatures that lived under there and how wondrous it'd be to swim with them. One day I managed to step a toe into the water, and then I went in up to my knees and my waist, until I could hold my own. We swam every day after that."

"She sounded amazing."

"She was." Gwen looked up at him. "She always told me I could do anything I set my mind to, and that I shouldn't listen to naysayers."

"She'd be proud of you."

"You think so?"

"You're a successful businesswoman and a talented artist. Your work is going to be featured in one of the best museums in the world. You have friends who love you. You're kind and caring." He wiped a trail of tears from her cheek. "She's probably smiling down from heaven at you."

Gwen didn't say anything for a while, as if she were letting his words sink in. Then she kissed his shoulder. "Thank you."

Gwendolyn fell asleep in his arms, but Rick was wide awake. His thoughts bugged him.

No, not his thoughts—his feelings. Because it was entirely possible that he *liked* Gwendolyn Pierce. The kind of like that led to picket fences and station wagons.

He never took himself for a picket fence kind of guy.

He looked down at her, nestled on his shoulder, sleeping like a princess, and something in him eased. It was okay—Gwendolyn wasn't a picket fence kind of woman either.

Glancing at the time, he wondered if he should go home. It was late and they'd never spent the night together.

He didn't really want to go. He was perfectly happy right where he was.

But he knew he should, so he eased himself from under her, pausing to soothe her back into sleep when she roused. Silently he dressed and padded into the kitchen for a glass of water before leaving.

Taking a glass from the cabinet, he walked to the freezer. This was where he found out she was a serial killer, because all serial killers kept their trophies in the freezer. He grinned as he opened the door, picturing being faced with bulging eyes and plastic bags of random body parts.

What he found was worse than a cut-up body. It was stacks and stacks of hundred dollar bills.

Chapter Sixteen

LOLA SHOVED OPEN the door, the usually delicate chimes agitating sharply. "Gwen, close up shop! We're going to Eve's."

Gwen shut the notebook where she was doodling her name entwined with Rick's to avoid the interrogation she'd expect. "Why are we going to Eve's?"

"Chocolate croissants." Her friend grinned. "Just out of the oven."

"You had me at croissant." She hopped off the chair and slipped into the shoes she'd discarded earlier. Anything to distract her from wondering why she hadn't seen Rick in almost a week—not since that evening he'd comforted her after Mamie Yvette's death.

Not wanting to dwell on either fact, she grabbed her sweater because the fog had blown in that afternoon and followed an energetic romance writer out of the store.

"Have you been eating cookies again?" Gwen asked as she locked the door.

Lola laughed, bouncing on her toes. "I went to Bikram today. I've still got the endorphin rush from being baked into a living pretzel."

"I tried yoga once." It'd been in India, where she'd traveled for several months.

"I can't see you doing yoga," Lola said, slipping her arm through Gwen's as they walked down the street. "You're always on the move. If you were a character in one of my books, I'd write in a tragic past you were trying to run away from."

Since that was a little close to home, she said, "How's your book coming along?"

Lola perked up. "Great, actually. I wrote fifteen pages so far today. I had some trouble earlier this week, but I firmed up my heroine's motivation and now the story's rolling. I should be done way before my deadline."

"Bikram and fifteen pages. You really deserve a chocolate croissant."

"I hear you've been busy too."

Gwen glanced at her friend. Did she mean Rick? Lola didn't really know Rick.

"With the de Young exhibit. Eve told me."

"Oh. Yes." She tried to smile. It felt more like a wince. She'd signed all the contracts in a moment of rebellion. It'd been easier to do after her old picture had been all over the Internet again. No one had come up to her and accused her of being the erstwhile Grape Princess. She figured she was safe enough, as long as she took some care.

Still, after having been so wary all these years, it'd been a leap. The first few days after she signed the releases, she kept looking over her shoulder, waiting for paparazzi to descend—or worse: Gautier de la Roche. Who had a vested interest in keeping her lost.

"Here we are." Lola gave her a sly look as she pushed open the door to Grounds for Thought.

Gwen shook her head at her friend. "Why are you acting so—"

"*Congratulations!*"

She stopped short, shocked still by the balloons and people standing toward the back. "What?"

Lola prodded her forward. "To celebrate your commission to the de Young, silly."

"Oh." She walked into the cheering crowd, accepting their well wishes. Eve held out glasses to her partner Treat, who was filling them with champagne. Maggie, Eve's barista, passed around a tray of mini pastries to other friends from the neighborhood. Olivia stood smiling at her proudly.

But no Rick.

She forced her smile to stay affixed on her face, but it was difficult. Why wasn't he here?

She hadn't seen him in days—since that night he'd comforted her. He'd slipped out in the night, leaving a note for her saying he was going to be busy this week.

That was it.

Too busy to call her? Or text?

Since that night, she'd been useless. All she'd done all week was listen to sappy love songs and smell the pillow he'd slept on.

She was so pathetic.

"Congratulations, Gwen." Eve thrust a glass of champagne in her hand and then gave her a quick half-hug.

Gwen blinked at all the people and the decorations. "You didn't have to do this."

"Of course we did. We're proud of you." Eve leaned in and whispered. "I made those chocolate pastries you like so much, but don't worry if you don't get enough. I saved a batch for you to take home."

She laughed. "Thank you."

"You deserve this and so much more," Olivia said as she joined them. She gave Gwen a big squeeze. "We wanted to celebrate with you."

"I couldn't have asked for a better surprise." Except maybe if Rick were here too, she amended silently.

"I only wish I could have remembered that reporter's name. I'd have invited her to cover this, too. I'm so spacey these days." Olivia touched her stomach. "Hormones gone wild."

Gwen stared at her friend's belly, not understanding. Then she saw the sparkling water in Olivia's hand and gasped. "Are you pregnant?"

Beaming, Olivia held her stomach protectively. "Yes. Four months. And he's healthy."

She grabbed her friend in a hug. A long time ago, Olivia had miscarried a baby and she'd blamed herself for the loss. Gwen knew this had to be both triumphant and scary.

Just then the front door burst open and Olivia's husband Michael stormed in. He walked straight to

his wife, eyes only for her. He kissed her hello, touching her belly reverently.

Gwen backed away, feeling like an intruder.

A jealous intruder.

If only Rick looked at her like that. If only Rick had shown up.

Having her glass topped off, she wandered through the small crowd, stopping to thank everyone who congratulated her, making her way to the back patio. She needed air—a moment to gather herself so she could be appropriately grateful for the party instead of pouty that one man hadn't come.

Gwen loved Eve's patio. It was so like her friend: to the point, practical, yet delightful. Lush plants surrounded wooden benches and tables. Half the patio was covered to protect against the fog that invariably crept in most afternoons. Tonight, the tiny white lights were on, making it look like a place where fairies lived. Magical. Romantic. The kind of place you'd want your lover to kiss you.

If he were there.

"Are you hiding out here?"

She whirled around, relaxing when she saw it was Treat. "It's a good hiding place."

"Eve would still find you." He gave her that slow, sexy grin he had.

And, oddly, it wasn't nearly as affecting as Rick's smug smirk. She frowned. She would *not* ask about Rick, even if Treat was his best friend and was likely to know where he was.

"Rick would find you too," Treat said as if reading her mind.

She shook her head. "I don't know about that."

"Rick and I have been friends since college," he said after a moment. "Rick's always been around the baser part of humanity. Cheating husbands and wives and swindling people. But at least he had his parents as an example of love. At the core, even if he's skeptical, he believes it exists. He values truth and honesty above all."

And she was a liar, because she couldn't tell him the truth of her background, and that brought her down. "Why are you telling me this?"

"I think you know why." He smiled gently at her. "You know you can trust him."

Could she?

Yes. The answer came strong and without question. She nodded and then impulsively hugged Treat.

"Thank you."

"For the record, I've known him a long time, and I've never seen him so disturbed by a woman. He loves a puzzle, and usually he's figured out a person in no time. It's not often someone keeps him guessing." Treat chucked her under her chin. "Keep up the good work."

Except that keeping him guessing meant keeping up the lies.

But then she heard her grandmother's voice in her head: *Trust love, Geneviève. Love will always prevail.*

Her grandmother had always been right. Gwen just had to trust that Rick cared enough to stick with her after he knew all her secrets.

Chapter Seventeen

"Son," RICK'S FATHER Duncan yelled into the receiver, "your mother is driving me crazy. You still have a futon at your office?"

Rick tried to imagine his dad, who was just as tall but twice as wide, fitting onto the futon in the other room. "How do you feel about your feet dangling?"

"If it'll save my marriage I'm all for it."

"What did you do this time?"

His dad blustered and bellowed, but everyone knew he was all bark and no bite. "Why are you accusing *me*? That woman is the problem here. I was just watching Elsie Harding's window out of professional curiosity. I can't help if the woman traipses in her house *au naturel*."

Rick shook his head. Ever since his dad retired a couple years ago, it'd sparked strife at home. Not so much that Rick worried about his parents' marriage, but he wouldn't be surprised if his mom chased the old man with a cast iron pan. "You know you're welcome here any time, Dad, but shouldn't you work on the basic problem and do some part time work?"

Duncan sighed. "I promised your mother I'd take her to St. John. But I do miss the thrill of the chase."

He decided not to point out that most of a private detective's time was spent waiting and watching. There was no thrill. If you wanted excitement, you had to get it someplace else.

He'd found it with Gwendolyn.

He snorted. Did he ever. She had enough money to buy a small country, housed in her freezer. That was pretty exciting.

"Son," his dad barked. "Where's your head? I asked you about your cases three times."

"Sorry. I was thinking."

"Humph." There was silence on the other end.

Silence where his father was concerned was never a good idea. "Dad—"

"You met a girl."

"Why do you automatically go there? What if it's a client that's giving me trouble?"

"No, this is woman trouble. You want to know

how I deduce this?"

"Do I have a choice?"

His dad ignored him. "One—"

Sighing, Rick leaned back in his chair and propped his feet on the desk.

"—you're distracted. Not in a work-related way," his father interjected quickly, "but in an I've-got-the-blues sort of way. And you're moping."

"I'm not moping," he protested.

"Do I look like an idiot? And you better not ask your mother that." He continued. "Two, you've been busy the past couple months. I call you at home and you're not there."

"How do you know?"

"Because if you were, you'd answer the phone."

Rick couldn't deny that. "And three?"

"Three, *you* called *me*. The only time you ever call me is when you have trouble with a case or with a woman, and if it's a case you mention that right off." His dad laughed, sounding triumphant at having solved a puzzle.

"I'm glad you're so gleeful about this, Dad." He shook his head, wishing he could find the hilarity in that too. But he had the image of that money burned in his mind. Add to that Olivia's pissed voice in his head, telling him he was a jerk for missing Gwen's party, and it left him distinctly humorless.

And — the most absurd part of this all — he *missed* her. He missed her strange logic and funky curls. He missed the bright light in her eyes and the way she blazed through life. He missed the feel of her in his arms, talking to him.

Telling him lies.

"What's going on, son? Maybe I can help you."

Frustrated, he sat up. "It's just there are things about herself she hasn't told me."

"Have you asked?"

He blinked. "What?"

"Have. You. *Asked*?" his dad said slowly, like he was slow.

And maybe he was. "Actually, I haven't."

"But you've pried and poked and theorized behind her back." Duncan hummed. "That's our way, but remember one of the cardinal rules of getting information is asking for what you want. It's the easier route, and eight times out of ten you'll get it."

"Dad, your intellect is underrated."

"Tell your mother that. Now go get your girl."

"Dad?"

"Yes?"

"Thanks."

Rick all but raced to Outta My Gourd. On the way, he made a mental list of all the things he was going to ask her—the freezer-full of money at the very top. He burst into the store, slightly out of breath but determined.

Gwendolyn came running from the back, her big eyes even wider. When she saw him, she put a hand to her chest. "You scared me. I thought I was being raided."

He walked straight to her, hauled her in his arms, and kissed her. It wasn't in his script, but his gut told him it was the right way to go.

She melted against his body instantly, even though he got the sense she didn't want to.

He couldn't blame her. Raising his head, he lifted her chin and said, "First of all, I'm sorry I missed your party. Olivia's told me I'm a bastard, but it wasn't something I hadn't realized on my own."

She nodded solemnly, but her eyes lightened a little. "Thank you."

"I was angry at you, because we've been seeing each other for weeks and I feel like I don't know you." He thought about the money in the refrigerator. "You hide yourself away from me. The only time you're really honest is in bed, like that night you told me about your grandmother."

Gwendolyn glanced away. A long time elapsed, and he started to feel disappointment deep in his chest. She wasn't going to trust him.

Then she nodded. "You're right."

He shook his head. He must have misunderstood. "Excuse me?"

"You're right," she said more surely. She took his hand, her chin determined. "Are you free now?"

"Yes."

"I have something I want to show you."

Was she going to show him how she robbed a bank? But he knew better than to let his sarcasm taint the moment so he simply let her lock up the shop and direct him where to go.

Which turned out to be the Mission. Specifically, the Purple Elephant: A Creative Place for Kids.

He frowned at the entrance. Was the money in her refrigerator tied to this place?

Gwendolyn faced him before they entered. She looked up at him with clarity that was honest. "This is a small place to start, but it's close to my heart. I began this charity with the help of a few people I'd met over the years. It was actually the reason I came to San Francisco in the first place. I started it because — "

"You thought all kids should learn to paint happy little trees?" he asked.

She smiled. "Precisely."

"I read on the website that you were one of the founders." At her shocked look, he shrugged. "That was before we declared a détente."

"It better have been." She gave him a look that meant business and then sashayed ahead of him into the building.

It was exactly how he'd have expected it to be, knowing Gwendolyn. Bright, busy, and loud with laughter. She took his arm and pointed. "Over there is a sketch class. Next to it, where you see the easels, is what we call free painting. We set up the easels and an assortment of different mediums and let them at it. In the other corner, we have what I call tactile arts."

"Which is...?"

"Clay. Yarn, for knitting or whatever. Fabric and

stuff if someone wants to sew. Materials for building models." She shrugged. "That sort of thing."

"Are these all underprivileged kids?"

"Not at all." He curls bounced she shook her head so vigorously. "We don't discriminate. Especially against economic standing. Everyone should have a chance to create, if they want, regardless of where he or she comes from. Sometimes the more money you have, the more stifled you become."

He faced her. "Who stifled you as a kid? And did you steal his money?"

She stepped back on a gasp, eyes wide. "What do you mean?"

He closed the gap, lowering his head to softly say, "I saw the money in your freezer, Princess."

Her eyes narrowed, and she grabbed him by his jacket to yank him close. Her voice was an outraged hiss. "You *snooped*?"

"No, I was getting ice." He shook his head. "I almost wish I didn't see it, but I can't forget it exists. Tell me you didn't do anything illegal."

"Of course I didn't, you idiot." She glared at him. "How could you even think that?"

He leaned in and whispered, aware of the looks

they were getting. "How could I think otherwise? You never tell me anything about yourself. You're one big, blank canvas. You could be anything. That's what I was saying."

She looked like she wanted to argue, but then she deflated. "You're right."

"I am?" he asked suspiciously.

"Yes." She stared him straight in the eye. "I promise it's not illegally gained, that every cent of it's mine, and I'll explain where it came from. Where *I* came from. But not today."

"When?"

She winced. "I've been guarding it for a long time. I'm afraid if I talk about it, that if it leaves my mouth the wrong ears will hear."

He held her arms gently but securely. "Are you in trouble?"

"No." But there was a hint of hesitation to the answer.

"Okay," he agreed reluctantly. "I'll wait, but not long."

"I'll tell you," she promised with a whisper.

He wasn't sure what it said about him that he believed her. He took her hand, so there wouldn't be any distance between them. She relaxed, a wondrous look lighting her face, and kissed his fingers.

"Gwen!"

They both turned.

A gangly girl came bounding at them from the backroom. She was all legs and teeth, smiling happily at Gwendolyn. Her hair was in a bouncy ponytail and she wore a plaid shirt and skinny jeans.

"Hey there!" the teenager called out, charging them. She threw her arms so enthusiastically around Gwendolyn that he let go of her and put his hand at her back to brace her.

Gwendolyn returned the girl's tight hug. "Why the enthusiasm?"

"Because I finished the volunteer signup calendar on the website and it *rocks*. You can even color-code it by type of class. I've got skills." The girl looked at him like an interested puppy dog. "Who are you?"

He reached out his hand. "Rick, a friend of Gwendolyn's."

He didn't miss the inquiring way look the girl gave Gwendolyn. He expected her to shy away or dismiss him—the way teenagers usually acted. So he was impressed when she took his hand, looked him in the eye, and said, "I'm Laurel. I work here."

"You don't work here," Gwendolyn corrected. "You're a student."

The girl snorted. "Only in my dad's mind."

Shaking her head, Gwendolyn faced him. "Her dad thinks that she's taking art classes."

"I failed art last year," the girl said proudly.

"She's abysmal at drawing, but she's excellent at anything technical. She built our website and runs everything around it. It's an amazing thing, but her dad doesn't know." Gwen shook her head. "Tell her she should tell him. He's going to be as proud of her as we are."

Laurel snorted again.

"You're better off telling him. It's no good keeping secrets." He glanced at Gwendolyn. "They end up coming out in the end, and it's always harder."

Her narrowed gaze promised him retribution.

The teenager looked between them. "You guys are talking to each other but you aren't saying anything." Then she gasped. "Are you Gwen's boyfriend?"

Before he could say anything, Gwendolyn said, "We don't like to label things."

Laurel nodded knowingly. "Kind of like how losers don't like to be called losers."

"Something like that," Gwen said, trying to hide a smile.

The girl turned to him. "If you were an animal, what would you be?"

Rick arched a brow at Gwendolyn, who just shrugged. Turning back to Laurel, he said, "A panther."

"Huh." The girl's nose wrinkled as she studied him. "I'd have pegged you for a giraffe."

Gwendolyn snickered. He silently promised her retribution.

Laurel continued, oblivious. "Rick, if you were a crayon color, what would you be called?"

He looked straight at Gwen. "Shocking orange."

"I don't think that's a color," the girl said, frowning.

Obviously also remembering their poolside interlude, Gwendolyn's face was bright red. "That's enough, Laurel," she said in a reasonably decent adult voice.

"I'm just trying to determine if he's a good fit for you." She shrugged. "But whatev. Live your own life."

She shrugged and flounced off. Then she whirled around. "But if you want my opinion, he's perfect." She grinned and then skipped off.

Gwen faced him, lowering her voice again. "We're building a closet to lock her in."

"She can't be all that bad. She thinks I'm good for you."

Gwendolyn rolled her eyes in a perfect imitation of the teenager.

He took her hand again. "We're good when we decide we're on the same side."

"Are we on the same side?" She looked up at him.

"Yes." Then because there was a moment of doubt and because he wanted to be honest, especially with her, he said, "At the moment."

"Yes." She nodded. "At the moment, *this* moment is great."

He brushed her hair from face. "I can't argue with that."

Chapter Eighteen

"You're brooding into your coffee, Camille," Elizabeth said as she breezed into the kitchen. "You know it disrupts my chi when you brood."

She was always doing something that disrupted her mother's chi. Her mother had missed the free love era of Northern California — British punk rock had formed her early years. She'd never been so much about going with the flow as she'd been about screw the establishment. But a couple years ago she'd interviewed the Dalai Lama and ever since she'd been all about her chi. Unfortunately, she wasn't so much about her chi that she meditated. Elizabeth thought it'd ruin her edge.

Camille had always wished Elizabeth was more a mother and less edgy. She sighed and returned her attention to her computer. Not that staring at the screen any longer would produce a miracle.

Her mother gestured toward her. "Why are you dressed that way?"

"This?" She looked down at the dress she'd bought specially for her first date with Dylan. It was a splash of color, a pink so bright Gwendolyn Pierce would have been proud. Camille wouldn't have chosen it but the saleslady assured her it looked great on her. It felt great. And Dylan hated her in black.

"It's hideous." Elizabeth took a cereal bowl out of the sink and tapped ashes from her cigarette into it. "Since when do you get dressed up to work from home?"

She hadn't been planning on working, but she'd gotten ready early—it was this or get worked up and nervous about the date. "I'm not dressed up," she said, moving her feet further under the table so her mother wouldn't see the whimsical lacy pink shoes she'd splurged on to match.

"If you weren't so focused on your computer, I'd say it was that outfit that was causing you such consternation." Her mother arched her brow at the laptop as she took a puff. "What are you doing that's causing you trouble?"

"It's nothing." Elizabeth would only laugh if

Camille told her she was researching a missing Grape Princess out of a hunch that the woman was underground as a gourd artist in Laurel Heights.

But then why had Gwendolyn reacted the way she had when she'd seen the article on Yvette de la Roche? Camille kept coming back to that — and the coincidence between the similarity between Geneviève and Gwendolyn.

"It's not nothing," her mother said, putting out the cigarette. "You have that constipated look on your face."

She touched her cheeks. "What?"

Elizabeth waved at her. "You've always gotten that look when something was vexing you. Tell me what it is."

"It's really nothing." Because that was what she'd yielded so far. There wasn't anything to definitively connect Gwendolyn to the wine heiress, despite the feeling she'd had.

"Just tell me, for God's sake." Her mother sat down across from her. "I'm not going to burst your little bubble."

Elizabeth said that now, but she always managed to do it regardless. But Camille had nothing to lose.

What could it hurt? "I was interviewing this woman for an article, and during the session I got the sense that she wasn't all she seemed."

Her mother leaned forward, suddenly interested. "How do you mean?"

"I had a feeling she was hiding something." Camille shrugged, trying to downplay. It sounded ridiculous.

"Always listen to your gut, Camille. It's the first rule of journalism. What set off your instincts?"

"I had this newspaper in my hand"—she picked up the now-ratty paper and handed it to her mother—"and she got really upset when she saw the article on Yvette de la Roche."

Her mother snatched the paper out of her hand and scanned it. "I remember when Yvette de la Roche's granddaughter went missing. It was the biggest news of the year."

"I don't know why I thought there might be a connection," she said to downplay her guess. "It just seemed like her reaction to the article was severe."

"What does this woman look like?"

She thought about wacky, colorful Gwendolyn Pierce and shook her head. "Not anything like the photos of Geneviève de la Roche I've seen."

"Are they close to the same age?"

"I don't know how old Gwendolyn is."

Her mother's laser stare focused on her. "Gwendolyn?"

"Yes."

"Gwendolyn. Geneviève." She arched her brows meaningfully. "Coincidence?"

"There's no such thing as coincidence," Camille parroted automatically. "It's what set off my trigger to begin with."

"Exactly." Her mother slapped the paper on the table, stood up, and began to pace. "Do you realize the potential here? You'd have the biggest story of the year if you've found the missing Grape Princess."

"But I can't find conclusive information."

Her mother lunged into the seat next to her and shifted the laptop to face her. Scrunching her forehead, she leaned forward. "Go get my glasses, Camille."

She glanced at the time. Elizabeth, when she got focused, could suck up hours in the blink of an eye. Camille didn't have hours—she was supposed to meet Dylan in forty-five minutes for their first date.

"Can we do this another time? I have someplace I'm supposed to be."

Her mother glared. "What could be more important than the biggest story of the year?"

She opened her mouth to say Dylan, but she couldn't. Her mother would ridicule her for putting her social life before her profession.

Elizabeth arched her brow. "Well?"

Camille knew better than to say anything when her mother took that tone, so she got up and went to the study. It took a few minutes until she found them in the chaos of the workspace.

Before she returned to the kitchen, she pulled out her cell and called Dylan.

"Camille," he said, simply, when he answered the phone. "I'm impatient to see you."

She shivered at the pleasure and promise in his voice. For a second, she was tempted to just walk out and leave her mother hanging.

"*Camille*," Elizabeth called from the kitchen. "Did you get lost?"

"Camille?" Dylan said.

She drooped and kicked off her shoes. They were uncomfortable anyway. "That's why I was calling. I need to cancel our date."

The silence from his end was jarring.

"I'm sorry," she said quickly. "Something came up, and I can't make it."

"I see."

The disappointment in his voice broke her heart. "Dylan —"

"It's okay. I really do understand, Camille. I'm not happy about it, but I understand."

"Maybe we can set up another time?" she asked tentatively.

There was a long silence on the other end. She was positive he was going to say *No*. She began to feel a black hole of despair in the pit of her stomach just as he finally said, "Another time. We'll talk when you're not busy with your mother."

"*Camille*," her mother yelled.

Practically collapsing in relief, Camille nodded, not caring that he couldn't see. "Okay, good. I'll talk to you later?"

"Yes," he said. "You better go before Elizabeth turns into a dragon."

Hanging up, feeling a little better, she padded to the kitchen.

Her mother was hunched over the keyboard, an unlit cigarette in her mouth, fingers tapping furiously. "About time you found them."

Camille held out the glasses. "Here you go."

Elizabeth grunted, making no move to take them. "Have you checked Gwendolyn Pierce with any sources at the FBI?"

What sources? "Not yet."

"Think like a bloody journalist, Camille." Her mother scowled. "Have you run her fingerprints?"

"I don't have any."

"Well perhaps you should get some." Elizabeth snapped the laptop shut. "I'd swear you were switched at birth if I hadn't had you at home."

Ouch. She winced as her mother walked out of the kitchen.

But Elizabeth was right—she wasn't stepping up and thinking like a journalist. She was acting like a sullen teenager who wanted to go out with the boy. Her career was more important—Dylan cared about her and understood.

She stared at the photo of Geneviève de la Roche on her computer screen. How was she going to get fingerprints?

The gourd.

She had to go pick up the gourd she'd made with Gwendolyn—it'd have the woman's fingerprints. So she'd just need to find a way to compare it to Geneviève de la Roche's fingerprints.

That was where it helped to have a friend who was a thriller writer.

A friend who also wanted to take her on a date.

She smiled slowly, feeling more positive than she had in a long time. Everything was going to work out. She could feel it.

Camille was waiting outside Outta My Gourd for Gwen when she arrived Friday morning.

The artist arched her brow as she rolled up to the front door. "I'm experiencing déjà vu."

Clearing the nerves from her throat, Camille said, "I came to pick up the gourd I made."

"Ah." Gwendolyn unlocked the door and waved her in. "Make yourself at home. I'll be right out."

She murmured something and tried not to fidget too much. She had so much riding on this, it was hard to sit still. What if there wasn't a good fingerprint?

Kate Perry

What if Dylan wouldn't help her? What if his contact at the CIA didn't glean anything?

What if she was right and had found the Grape Princess?

Taking a shuddering breath, she wiped her palms on her skirt.

"Here you go."

Nearly jumping out of her skin, she whirled around.

Gwendolyn held the gourd Camille had made in her hand, studying it critically. "This is really nice work."

"It is?" she asked doubtfully.

"I wouldn't say that if I didn't mean it." The woman took it to the counter and wrapped it up. "What are you going to do with it?"

"Um. I'm giving it to a friend." She tried not to feel guilty about the thinly veiled truth but failed.

"Good. Art should be appreciated, especially when it's given out of love."

"Oh, I don't love him," she said quickly, only those words felt like a lie as well.

"Hmm."

Camille frowned. "What does that mean?"

Gwendolyn shrugged. "Whatever you want it to mean. Here you go."

She took the bag from the woman, feeling as though it was a time bomb. "Thank you," she murmured as she walked out of the store.

The second she was down the street, she pulled out her phone and called Dylan.

He answered on the first ring. "I was just thinking about you."

The way he said it, low and whispery, like he'd just woken up and was still lying in bed, made her squirm. She tried not to go there, instead clearing her voice and saying, "I need a favor."

"Ask me."

"I need some fingerprints run. Do you think one of your CIA contacts can do it for me?"

There was a pause on the line. Then he said, "Are you okay?"

"It's for a story."

"That doesn't answer my question."

She looked at the bag. "I need to do this."

"I'm at home, Camille. Come here."

Hanging up, she decided to splurge on a cab. She gave the driver Dylan's address in the Mission.

He opened the door for her before she got all the way to his doorstep. He stood there wearing nothing but pajama bottoms. She hadn't realized men did that except in movies. He certainly looked like he'd stepped off the big screen—he was as hot as any actor out there.

Dylan watched her as she trudged up the last of the steps.

She couldn't tell what he was thinking, but that wasn't unusual—she often couldn't read his thoughts.

He, on the other hand, read her like an open book with humungous font. "What are you up to, Camille?" he asked as she stepped past him.

"I just need the prints on this"—she held out the bag—"run and compared to an international database."

"What for?"

"For a story."

He looked at her disbelievingly.

"Please." She tried to look like a puppy dog.

It worked. He took the bag from her. "What about your writing? I thought you were going to focus on a story."

"This *is* about my writing."

"No, this is about your mother."

"What?" She recoiled, feeling like she'd been struck from out of the blue.

He set the bag down without taking his eyes from her. "Do you remember when we met?"

"Of course I do."

"You were just graduated from college," he said, "and when you glommed on to me I thought you were looking for a father figure."

She flushed. "I didn't think of you like that. Ever."

"No, because it isn't Daddy's approval you want. It's Mommy's."

Automatically she began to deny that, but how could she? She closed her mouth and crossed her arms.

"But you know what, Camille? Mommy is never going to give you what you want, because she can't see who you are."

"And you can?"

"*Yes*." He stepped up to her, so close she could feel the warmth of his body. "You're not a journalist. You're a storyteller. Journalism is too dry for you. You're lush and layered. Underneath all that black, you're colorful and creative. You're the antithesis to

235

Elizabeth Bernard, and you're going to be unhappy if you don't accept that."

She shook her head. "At one time, I'd have agreed with you, but my journalistic instincts have finally kicked in."

He groaned and threw his hands in the air.

"No." She lowered his arms. "Listen. I'm onto something here, and I need your help, Dylan. Please?"

He said nothing.

"*Please*, Dylan?"

Dylan studied her, his thoughts veiled. Finally, he said, "Is this really what you want?"

"Yes," she said with more confidence than she felt.

"And what about us?"

"Us?" She shook her head, confused. "What about us?"

"That's what I thought." He turned away. "Fine. I'm done."

Panic caught in her throat. "What?"

"I'm done, Camille." He faced her, arms crossed. "I'll call you as soon as I hear from my contact, and then that's it."

She wanted to say that was all she needed, but she knew she wasn't talking about her favor — he was talking about them.

Swallowing the sense that she was losing something precious, she started to ask him what she could do to change that — to strike a bargain. Only based on his expression, he wasn't in the mood to negotiate. Afraid she'd say something that'd make him change his mind, she shut her mouth and nodded.

Her inside self was kicking her, telling her that if she walked out right then, she'll have screwed up the most important thing in her life.

Your career is the most important thing, she heard her mother's cold voice say.

She just wasn't sure right then. Confused, she thanked him again and left, trying not to give power to the doubts that churned inside her.

Chapter Nineteen

RICK HAD LOOKED so haggard when he'd arrived at her apartment that Gwen took his hand and led him directly to Candace's pool. She felt gratified when he sighed, long and heartfelt, as he slipped into the water.

She did a few vigorous laps with him before she slowed down to an indolent pace. She watched him continue, lap after lap, going all out, admiring his muscular grace.

He came to a sudden stop, shaking his head and looking for her.

She smiled at him from the edge where she floated. When he joined her, she hugged him like a koala. "Did you work out whatever was bothering you?" she asked.

"Yes. Thanks." He pushed her hair back. "I don't think I said hello to you properly."

"You didn't."

"I should take care of that."

"You should."

The kiss began soft and gentle, heating slowly until she was more out of breath than the laps had left her.

Rick pressed his forehead to hers and sighed. "I needed that. Both the laps and you."

She rubbed his shoulders. "Tough day at work, honey?"

His lips quirked. "You could say that. I was hired to find a man who'd ducked out on his family. I found him today."

"Where is he?"

"Peru."

Gwen winced. "That's not good for the mother or the child, is it?"

"Not at all." His jaw tightened. "The bastard cleaned out the bank accounts before he left."

Gautier de la Roche had had many faults, but at least he'd never have turned his back on her, even when he knew she wasn't his biological child. "Are you going to fly down there and castrate him?"

"I wish." Taking a deep breath, he lifted his face

to the moon. "I just feel bad for the mother."

"And the child."

Rick floated onto his back, holding her on top of him. "I don't know. Isn't it better not having a father than having one who's a jerk?"

She considered that seriously. "Good point."

"You sound like you're speaking from experience."

It was instinct to change the subject to something frivolous and light, but she'd promised him openness and honesty. She had to try. She wanted to try.

She trusted him, she realized with a start.

Shaking her head, she said carefully, "My father can't be blamed for the way he treated me."

Under her, Rick stiffened. "How did he treat you?"

"With disregard. He had Roger, my brother, the firstborn and heir. Roger's also his rightful child. I'm not. My mother had me through an affair and took every opportunity to rub it in his face." She wrinkled her nose. "That makes my mother sound awful, but really she was just unhappy and acting out. She and my father were never very close. He had affairs, so she had them, too, in retaliation."

"Do you know who your real father is?"

"No. I can't say I don't wonder about it, but it

becomes less important the older I become."

Rick looked like he was processing the information. Finally he said, "You didn't deserve any of that."

She shrugged. "It made me who I am."

"Is that why you left?"

She shook her head but didn't clarify. That wasn't something she wanted to get into right then.

"My parents are loving," he said, holding her loosely. "They drive each other crazy sometimes, but they're a unit. A team. That's never been in question."

"I can't imagine that. It must be nice to have someone you can depend on," she said wistfully. Her parents had been petty and selfish.

"That's what I want." He gazed at her like she was the only thing that existed in the world. "When I pick the person I'm going to be with forever, I want it to be someone I can trust, who'll be as caring of me as I am of her."

She swallowed. "You expect to stay with someone forever?"

"Yes," he said unequivocally. "I want a relationship like my parents'. They have their ups and downs but in the end they always have each other's back."

She tried to picture it. It was hard but not impossible. With Rick, it wasn't impossible at all. "But where would we live?" she wondered out loud.

"My place," he said without hesitation.

She narrowed her eyes. "Is it all brown with leather and shag? With floor-to-ceiling mirrors in your bedroom?"

"I didn't realize you'd been over." He grinned. "I'd let you redecorate."

"You would?"

"As long as you don't touch the mirrors."

She splashed him. "We'd have to negotiate before I even considered leaving a toothbrush there."

"Like?"

"Like don't expect me to cook. It's not going to happen."

He shrugged. "I'll do the cooking then."

She slipped under water, she was so surprised. "You cook?"

"Mom made sure I learned. She said she was thinking ahead to the woman I'd live with one day."

"Clever woman."

"You don't even know. I wouldn't do my own laundry, so when I was thirteen she 'accidentally' washed my white clothes with red socks."

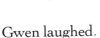

Gwen laughed.

"Sure, it's funny to you, but my pink underwear was a joke in the locker-room for weeks."

"You'd still look hot in pink underwear."

He perked up. "You think I look hot?"

"No, I just take pity on you by letting you get naked in my bedroom."

He dove for her, pulling her under. She came up laughing, entwined in him, glowing in the moonlight and the warmth of their dream.

Chapter Twenty

*T*HE STORY RAN on a Tuesday.

Camille sat on the stoop predawn, biting her nails as she waited for the newspaper to be delivered. She saw the newspaper truck half a block away, and she ran out to meet him.

The delivery guy looked at her like she was insane. If *his* professional life hung in balance over this article, he wouldn't have judged so harshly.

She ran inside, the paper clutched in her hand. When she'd turned in the article yesterday, along with the proof Dylan's source at the CIA had provided, Mac had flipped. After he stopped foaming at the mouth over the scoop of the decade, he'd quickly edited it and told her she was getting the front page. He told her it was sure to be syndicated, too.

Every reporter's dream.

If only she were happier about it.

Sitting at the kitchen table, she unwrapped the paper from the plastic and smoothed out the Daily in front of her. The front page read:

LOST GRAPE PRINCESS FOUND!

In smaller print, underneath, it said:

Story by Camille Bernard

She traced the letters with her finger. It looked amazing.

It felt... not as good.

"Is that it?" her mother asked strolling into the kitchen, her kimono fluttering around her. She snatched the paper from the table and held it up to read.

Camille held her breath. She put her hands under her seat so she wouldn't bite her nails in front of her mother.

It seemed like an eternity before her mother slapped the paper down on the table. She stood there like a Valkyrie, hands on her hips with a fierce expression on her face.

"That"—Elizabeth pointed to the discarded newspaper—"is worthy of a daughter of mine."

Hearing the validation didn't make her feel as

vindicated as she thought it would. Especially since Gwen had been so nice to her, when she'd obviously hadn't wanted anyone to find out who she was. Especially since she'd lost Dylan over it. "Thank you," she murmured.

Her mother leaned over the table. "You've finally come into your own. This calls for a celebration."

She should have felt like celebrating, but seeing the candid picture she'd taken of an unsuspecting Gwendolyn Pierce didn't make her feel as satisfied as she thought she'd be. "I don't know —"

"I do." Elizabeth clapped her hands and reached for the phone. "We're having a party."

"I don't really —"

"We're having a party, and that's the end of it." She frowned. "You're very glum for someone who scooped the biggest story of the year. You should be booking appearances on CNN and CNBC. Fame is fleeting, Camille. You need to make the most of it."

It was hard to make the most of it when your stomach was roiling with unhappiness.

Chapter Twenty-one

PEARL JAM'S CORDUROY blasted in the store. Gwen didn't often play such loud, enthusiastic music in the shop, but she needed something to match her mood.

It was a good mood. Buoyant. Exultant.

Blissful.

She sang along with the song. She felt happy whenever she heard it—it reminded her of a great weekend in Seattle with a couple she happened to meet. She'd started talking to the man named Eddie and his girlfriend at a café and they'd hit it off so well she ended up staying with them for a few days.

It wasn't until later that she found out who he really was.

The front door opened. She reluctantly turned the music down and turned to greet whoever it was. Her smile became genuine when she saw it was a good customer of hers who lived in the neighborhood. "Stacy. I haven't seen you in a while."

"We were in Europe. I've only been back a week, but I thought I should get in here before the masses."

Gwen looked around. What masses? But she shrugged it off.

"I want a commission. Something royal." Stacy giggled, wide-eyed with eagerness.

"Okay," she said hesitantly. "So you want purple? Or maybe something with a British flag?"

The woman patted her hand. "You'd know better than I do, sweetie. I just can't wait to tell my friends I commissioned a piece with you. When do you think it'll be done?"

"A couple weeks." That was new—that someone wanted to brag about having her artwork. Maybe the de Young article had come out. She needed to check.

"You'll call me? See you later." The woman waved, giggling delightedly, and headed out the door. As she left, there was a small commotion and Lola entered a second later.

Gwen was about to give her a perky hello when she saw her friend's face. "What happened?"

Lola simply set a newspaper down in front of her.

It took a moment before the headline registered.

Grape Princess Hiding in the Fog.

All the blood drained from her head.

"Sit." Lola stuck a stool under her and pushed her onto it. "Do you need water?"

She shook her head because she'd lost her ability to speak. She leaned forward, looking at the old picture of herself in black next to a new one she hadn't known had been taken. She slowly read the article below it.

It was all there. How she'd disappeared and shown up fourteen years later in San Francisco. It described her store and how she'd given up a socialite life to be an artist.

She slumped, stunned.

"Do I need to ask if it's true?" Lola asked.

She shook her head again.

"You're really Geneviève de la Roche? Is it okay if I'm excited about that? I've never met an heiress before."

"I'm not an heiress anymore. I'm a gourd artist."

"That's not what this article says." Lola tapped the paper. "This article says you just inherited a large chunk of your family's business when your grandmother passed away."

"I don't want it." Feeling a fire lit under her, she jumped up and began gesturing. "I left all that behind. I didn't want any of it then, and I definitely don't want any of it now."

"Was it that bad?"

"Worse. The games, the lies, the expectations and disappointments. It was poison." She jumped up, feeling as though something shocked her system. Waving her arms, she paced back and forth. "Then the media was there, cataloguing every mistake I made. It was suffocating me. I won't live that way again."

"But you're an adult now."

"The media never quits, and then there's my family." She gave Lola a dark look. "Now that Mamie Yvette is gone, her shares will be divided, and if she left any in my name, there'll be a tug-of-war to see who controls my interests. My father doesn't play fair. I'll be bloodied and left at the side of the road."

"And they tell me *I'm* dramatic." Frowning, Lola picked up the paper. "I can't believe you've been living anonymously all this time. It's amazing. I wonder how the reporter put two and two together though."

Gwen glared at the byline. "It's that reporter with the hungry eyes who did the article on the de Young.

And to think I helped her make a gourd."

Lola tapped the newspaper. "This is comprehensive. Something had to tip her off, or else maybe she found a source."

"No one knew anything—" She stopped abruptly. *Rick*.

"You thought of something. Or someone."

She'd told Rick details. If anyone were going to decipher the mystery of her, it'd have been him. He said he hadn't snooped into her things, but he *had* found her money.

A wave of desolation crashed over her. She dropped straight to the floor, landing on her butt.

"Gwen!" Lola crouched in front of her. "Are you okay?"

She shook her head. "I don't think I'll ever be okay ever again."

Lola got down and sat cross-legged on the floor next to her. "You know what we need to do? We need to brainstorm."

"No, we need to pack and leave." She frowned. "No, I'm not going to leave again. I've been running from them all this time. It's time to stop."

"Hell yeah it is." Her friend patted her on the leg.

253

"This is your home. It's time to stand your ground."

The phone began to ring. They both looked at it.

"Are you going to answer it?" Lola asked.

"No." It'd be press. Or worse: her family. "They're going to come for me."

"Nobody can make you do anything you don't want. Circumvent them."

"Excuse me?"

"Change the events." Lola shrugged. "Throw a wrench in their plans. Don't play their game. Do something they won't expect."

She blinked. "That may be brilliant."

"I know." Lola smiled, pleased with herself. She held out a hand.

Gwen took it and let her friend haul her up. Then she hugged her. "Thank you."

"Anytime."

The door opened for the second time in minutes. This time it was Rick.

A growl emerged from somewhere deep inside her. She clenched her fists, the bite of her nails the only thing grounding her. If Lola hadn't been there, she'd have lunged for his neck.

He must have sensed that because he stopped

abruptly. "Gwendolyn?"

"You bastard." She hissed, picked up a gourd, and threw it at his head.

Chapter Twenty-two

OF ALL THE reactions he'd expected when he walked into Outta My Gourd, having Gwen yell "You bastard!" as she beaned him with a pumpkin wasn't one.

Then again, the morning was full of all sorts of things he hadn't expected. Like finding out the woman he was interested in was a runaway wine heiress.

"I think I'll just leave not," Gwendolyn's blond friend said. She gave him a pitying look and hurried out of the store.

He hadn't even noticed her, and usually he noticed everything, especially an attractive blond. It was a testament to his state of mind.

Waiting until the blonde was gone, he turned to the Grape Princess. "When were you going to tell me?"

She made a sound that was halfway between a choke and a chortle—wholly humorless. "Why did

I need to tell you when you figured it out on your own?"

"I don't know what you're talking about."

She poked at the newspaper in his hand. "How else would they have gotten the story? Was there another private investigator following me around?"

"You think *I* outed you?" He gritted his teeth at the surge of anger.

"If the shoe fits." She grabbed a gourd from a table and moved it, setting it down so hard that he was surprised it didn't break in half. "You were so clever with all your talk of wanting honesty and hating deception, too. Well done, Clancy. You totally fooled me."

"You think I'd do that?"

"I don't have to think." She shoved a piece of art aside and glared at him or something. "I just hope you got enough money for your sacrifice."

"Sacrifice?"

"Well, yes. For sleeping with me." Her face hardened, but her eyes were pools of hurt.

He wanted to take her in his arms and reassure her as much as he wanted to shake sense into her.

"You performed really well, by the way," she added.

"Stop."

She stepped up to him. "I wouldn't have ever been able to tell you were doing it for information. You go above and beyond. Your clients must be thrilled with your results."

"Gwen, *stop*."

Her lips pouted, in that way they did when she was hurt but trying to hide it. "At least I can stop feeling bad for faking—"

He grabbed her and pressed his mouth to hers to stop her words.

She struggled against him, hitting his chest, but in the end she softened. Not completely, but enough. The kiss was passion incarnate, like always, but angry and desperate. Bitter.

She pushed him away. "Just go," she whispered. Eyes streaming, she walked dejectedly to the back.

He didn't follow her. Why should he when she didn't trust him? He turned around and walked out, slamming the door behind him as he tasted the saltiness of her tears on his lips.

Too agitated to go to the office, he stalked up and down the street a few times before going to Olivia's store.

She looked up when he walked in, her gaze tak-

Kate Perry

ing him all in. Without a word, she went to the front door, locked it, and returned to give him a big hug.

Olivia felt nice, but wrong. At all. She was too tall, too filled out. It seemed he preferred one particular elfin woman with a stubborn chin. He shook his head. Great.

"You looked like you needed that." She crossed her arms. "Assuming this is about Gwen."

"Do you know who she is?"

"Everyone who can read knows who she is." Olivia shook her head. "Who would have guessed? Other than you. You claimed she was hiding something all along."

He should have felt righteous for being right but he didn't. He felt angry because she could believe he'd betray her. "She thinks I outed her."

"Did you?"

He glared at her. "Of course not. How can you even ask?"

She shrugged. "You're the one who went around declaring you were going to uncover her secrets. She knew that."

He remembered the way he'd spied on her and winced.

"See?" Olivia arched her brow.

"She blames me."

"She would. What are you going to do about it?"

"Why should I do anything about it?"

"Because you love her."

He snorted.

Olivia rolled her eyes. "The clues are all in front of your eyes if you'd only open them."

"The only thing in front of my eyes is that Gwen lied to me about who she was."

"And who was that? That she was a caring, sensitive, artistic person? That she has a big heart and a penchant to enjoy life?"

"That she's an heiress."

"Because that negates everything else? Because you hate rich people? What?"

"No, because she *lied.*"

"She didn't lie about who she was." Olivia took him by the arms. "I saw the article this morning too, and just like you I was indignant that she'd deceived me. But two seconds later, when reason prevailed, I realized that she hadn't deceived anyone. Sure, there wasn't full disclosure about her family, but Gwen is who she always said she was. She's a bright, shiny, sweet friend who likes to paint squash."

"And if I'd conveniently withheld that I was a serial killer in my past?"

Olivia rolled her eyes. "You're being difficult."

"I'm being realistic. If you lie about one thing, you lie about everything."

"I'm telling you, Gwen never lied. She just didn't say she had a buttload of money." Olivia threw her hands in the air. "But fine. Cling to your hurts."

"Are you saying I'm being unreasonable in my anger? Because I think it's justifiable that I'm a little pissed."

"I don't." She pointed her finger at him. "And you know what? You need to get over it and realize what's important here."

"What is that?"

"Definitely not your pride. That's going to make you miserable and is going to be a poor companion in your old age. Gwen, on the other hand—"

"Geneviève," he corrected with an exaggerated French accent.

"*Gwen*," Olivia stressed, "is warm and funny. She'll be much better company as you get older. She'd at least keep you from becoming a crotchety old man."

He crossed his arms. He'd been imagining growing older with Gwen—at least he had been before all this. Not that he was going to admit that.

Olivia threw her hands in the air. "You're so dense. You know, most people only have one chance at love."

"Who said anything about love?"

"I did."

"You're just one of those people who's in love and wants everyone else in the world to be as happy."

"That's not true. Some people are too stupid to deserve love. I'm talking about you." She poked his chest. "The clues are all in front of your eyes, if you'd just open them and see."

He threw his hands in the air. "She lied to me, Olivia."

"What was she supposed to do? Confide in you? When you'd been such a bastard?"

He hadn't been a bastard to her—not after the beginning. He'd given her countless opportunities and openings to tell him.

That was what hurt.

Granted, she'd started to talk more about her past. He just wanted her to do it faster. If they'd had more time, would she have confided in him?

Kate Perry

He wasn't sure.

Olivia whacked his chest, dragging him from his thoughts. "Think about it. Don't screw this up."

He nodded, but he couldn't help thinking that it was hard to screw up something that was already so incredibly screwed up.

Chapter Twenty-three

"I CAN'T BELIEVE you're a princess," Laurel exclaimed for the hundredth time.

Gwen sighed and set aside the drawing she'd been working on. "I keep telling you, I'm not a princess."

"That's not what the newspapers are saying." The teenager sprawled on the beanbag next to her, looking introspective as she played with strands of her hair. "It's awesome, if you think about it. All girls want to be a princess, and you actually get to be one. Like, my little sister always wants to wear a tiara, but it's always those cheesy plastic ones. You get to have the real thing."

"No, I don't." Actually, her mother *had* bought her a tiara once. It's been ugly and uncomfortable. She'd gotten in big trouble when she threw it into the pond behind their house. "Don't tell me you want to be a princess."

"Heck no. I want to be an international skateboarding star and be on the cover of *Thrasher*."

"*Thrasher*?"

Laurel rolled her eyes. "A skateboarding magazine."

Gwen smiled faintly. "Am I being uncool?"

"Totally." The girl flopped onto her stomach. "So why'd you keep the whole princess thing hidden all this time? Because you want to be normal?"

"Exactly. If you saw all the reporters lined up outside my store, you'd understand." The newspaper people and photographers were camped outside Outta My Gourd. They hadn't found her flat, and unless some industrious person followed her, she didn't expect they would.

But being cooped up at home was overrated, so she'd been spending a lot of time at the Purple Elephant. It was only a matter of time before the media descended on her there, though.

"My mom was interviewed for a magazine a couple months ago," Laurel said. "The guy was a total jerk. He kept trying to look down her shirt. It was disgusting."

Gwen knew her mom was a big Internet mogul and, as the breadwinner, absent a lot, but that was the extent of her knowledge of the woman.

"So you just ran away?" Laurel put her chin in her hand, staring at Gwen. "And you've never gone back? Do you miss your family? I'd miss my sister if I up and left. I'd have to take her with me, even though she's a pain in the butt a lot of times."

"I—"

"Have they called you? This is totally like one of those TV shows where the person finds her long lost brother or something. And finds out she's super-rich." She gasped. "*Are* you super-rich? You'd have to be if you're a princess."

"I—"

"But you know what?" The teenager wagged a finger. "I don't think you're really a princess, because everyone knows Princesses like bling, and you are the un-blingy-est person ever."

She waited for the girl to continue, but Laurel just stared at her expectantly. "Are you finished?" she asked.

"Duh."

"No, I haven't been back. Yes, I'm probably somewhat rich. No, I don't like bling, or anything that goes with being rich, which is why I left."

"Then why'd you tell the press where you were?"

Trust a kid to get to the point. "I didn't."

"Who did?"

She thought about Rick, and her heart cracked a little more. "It's not something you need to worry about."

Not that Laurel was going to back down. Laurel was synonymous with *tenacious*. "Did you tell someone?"

She'd never told anyone anything—until Rick.

But she'd been wracking her brain, trying to remember if she let something slip that could tie her to the de la Roche empire. She'd mostly just told him about Mamie Yvette, but she'd been careful not to mention her grandmother's name or any identifying markers that could lead him to her family.

It was awful when she put it that way. That wasn't the way she wanted to live, especially with someone she lo—

She cut that thought off before it could form, but the echoes of the sentiment were resonating in her chest.

Was it possible?

She laughed humorlessly. Possible, likely, and

definitely. She'd felt *wretched* since she saw that article. Because of the beastly reporters — yes. But if she wanted to be honest, she was more miserable because she thought Rick betrayed her.

"You look like you're going to hurl," Laurel pointed out. "You're not, are you? Because I'll just leave if you are."

"No, I was just thinking about the person who sold me out to the media."

"Who was it?"

"Remember the guy I came in with that one time?"

"The *hawt* one?" she exclaimed, sitting up. "Tall dude? Leather jacket? Looked at you like he was going to eat you up?"

Gwen felt herself flush. "He did not."

"Yeah-huh, he did." The girl goggled at her. "You think *he* sold you out?"

"Well." She frowned. "Yes."

"No way." Laurel shook her head vehemently. "You're totally delusional."

"You talked to him for two seconds."

"And, apparently, in those two seconds I got to know him better than you do." The teenager looked at her with a combination of pity and scorn. "He was totally into you. He wouldn't have sold you out."

"But —"

"No, really. It was someone else, because that guy was *really* into you. Like, he'd totally learn how to skateboard for you, and he wouldn't stop until he was worthy."

Frowning, she tried to picture Rick on a skateboard.

Actually, she could, if it were important to her.

"He really didn't tattle on you. It had to be some-one else." Laurel tapped a finger to her lips. "Some-one who had something to gain."

Someone who had something vested, like a certain hungry-eyed reporter.

As soon as she thought it, she knew she had it right. She wasn't sure how she knew, but there wasn't a doubt in her mind. That day Camille Bernard had come in to pick up the gourd she'd made, she'd been acting strange.

The article had been released just days later.

"You thought of someone," Laurel said.

"Yes."

"You want me to go with you to talk to him?" The girl cracked her knuckles. "I've got a baseball bat."

Gwen's lips quirked. "Thanks, but I think I'm

okay handling it."

"And your boyfriend?"

She drooped. "I don't think he's my boyfriend anymore."

"He would be if you wanted him. He was pretty much drooling over you."

"No, he wasn't." Was he?

Laurel leaned forward, intense. "Do *you* like him? And I mean, the kind of like where you hug him even when he smells rank."

"He smells nice all the time," she replied without thought.

"See? You *like* him. You wouldn't *like* someone who didn't *like* you back." Under her voice, she added, "Unlike some people."

"Your parents?" Gwen asked sympathetically.

"You don't even know." The girl sighed dramatically.

She bet she did know, but that was a discussion for another day. For now... "You really think he likes me?"

"Dude," was all the girl said.

That seemed to sum it all up.

Chapter Twenty-four

CAMILLE WAS STARING unseeingly at a blank Word doc, wishing she could go home and bury herself in her covers, when a shadow fell over her desk.

She looked up to find a colorful gourd artist staring down at her.

Gwendolyn dropped a copy of the article on her desk. "Congratulations on your story. Well done. We need to talk."

Her nerves flared. "Should I have you frisked for weapons?"

"You should have thought about that before you printed that article." The woman turned and walked down the row of cubicles.

Hopping up, Camille hurried after her. The last thing she needed was an angry princess talking to Mac. Not that Mac would care—not when he was being patted on the back for "discovering" Camille.

She caught up with the woman. "There's a conference room this way."

Camille was aware of the curious stares they were getting, as well as the excited whispers when people recognized Gwendolyn. The woman just kept her head up, her bearing proud and strong.

It made Camille feel like crap.

She followed Gwendolyn into the conference room, taking the chair at the head of the table. Camille was tempted to sit all the way at the other end, but gathered her courage and sat next to her. It wasn't easy, because the bubbly gourd artist hadn't come. Today, the woman represented was powerful and in command. She could have been the CEO of a Fortune 500 company—or the heiress of a wine dynasty.

"It was you, wasn't it?" Gwen asked.

She didn't even pretend not to understand. "Yes."

"How did you figure it out?"

"A hunch." Wincing, she added, "And I had your fingerprints analyzed."

"The gourd." Gwen nodded thoughtfully. Then she leaned forward. "You don't know what you've done."

Camille swallowed. "I reported the truth. I didn't

report anything that wasn't the truth."

"You were reckless. You had power, and you abused it. You ruined a person's life."

A part of her withered, hearing that out loud, but she went with the justifications she'd been assuring herself with. "That's not the way I see it. You stand to gain millions, being back with your family."

"You don't have the complete story. Did you ever think to ask why I left?" Her gaze blazed with intensity. "Did you think that maybe my family was abusive, or that I'd been harmed in some way?"

She felt herself pale. "Were you?"

"Fortunately, no. But that could easily have been the reason. You assumed I left because I was a spoiled brat. Let me assure you a spoiled brat doesn't run away from money. In fact, if I were the person you painted in the article, I'd have run back the moment I found out I had an inheritance. My privacy was what was important, and you destroyed that."

There was truth to that. Camille didn't know what to say.

"I don't know why you locked on me and exposed my life in this way. I was harming no one. But whatever. That's not why I'm here."

She swallowed. "It's not?"

"No, I came to save you from yourself." Gwendo-lyn leaned across the table. "This isn't you, Camille."

Dylan had said the same thing. "How would you know who I am?"

"You're a gifted writer." She nodded to the news-paper. "The piece was beautifully written. Shouldn't you focus your talents on something that brings joy instead of ruining people's lives? Because that's an expensive price for your soul to pay."

The truth was one thing, but it was the look of kindness that killed Camille. She hunched in her seat, trying to protect herself from it. Only there was no evading it. "I don't understand why you're doing this."

"I don't either." Gwendolyn frowned. "I should have trashed your name all over the Internet and egged your car."

"I don't have a car."

"Then it's good I didn't waste my money on eggs." Gwendolyn stood up and started to walk out. Then she turned around. "My grandmother once told me that sometimes people were born into impossible sit-uations. That we need to break out of who we were and what we did to find who we really are. That's why I ran away, to find myself. To be happy."

It was a pretty speech, and Camille wanted to scoff at it, but even though Gwendolyn was angry there was a glow of contentedness to her, and that made Camille silent with jealousy.

Because she wasn't happy — not at all. She'd written the article, but it was a hollow victory because the one person she wanted to show it to wasn't returning her calls.

She didn't know if Dylan would ever call her back. Frankly, she couldn't blame him.

Impulsively, she turned to Gwen and asked, "It worked? It cured your unhappiness?"

Gwendolyn stood up, her gaze direct. "Of course it did. I discovered who I really was, and I found my true home. Not because I ran away, but because I walked away from the image everyone wanted to mold me into. Think about it."

Camille watched the woman leave, wondering if she had that much courage in her. *Wanting* to have that much courage.

Chapter Twenty-five

ER APARTMENT DOOR buzzed. Gwen's stomach fluttered with nerves, but she lifted her head, smoothed her skirt, and went to let them in.

Eve came in first, looking concerned, with Olivia following behind.

Gwen cleared her throat as she let them in. "Thank you for—"

Eve threw her arms around her and squeezed tight. "You poor thing!"

"Well. Okay," she said carefully. Looking over Eve's shoulder, she saw Olivia's caring, direct gaze. She searched for any sign of hurt or betrayal in it, relaxing when she didn't find anything more than sympathy. "You guys don't hate me?"

Eve's brow furrowed as she held Gwen at arm's length. "Why would we hate you?"

"Because I lied to you."

Olivia shook her head. "You didn't lie."

"I didn't?"

"No." Her friend smiled gently. "You didn't talk about your past, but you didn't misrepresent who you are. Did you?"

She wasn't Geneviève de la Roche any longer, in any shape or form. She'd left the Grape Princess behind ages ago. "I'm completely Gwendolyn Pierce."

"There you go." Olivia gave her a quick, hard hug and then let her go. "Why don't you make tea while Eve breaks out the madeleines she made."

Eve held up a little bag. "Chocolate chip."

They talked about inconsequential things as she made tea. They took everything into the living room and settled on the couch.

Olivia took her shoes off and tucked her feet under her. "Okay, tell us what happened."

She shook her head. "My grandmother convinced me to run away when I was twenty-one. I came into a trust fund, and she helped me devise a plan to withdraw the money and leave without anyone knowing where I went."

"Crazy," Eve said in awe. "I should have thought of that to get away from my dad. Except I didn't have a trust fund."

"Your dad isn't as bad as mine was, either." Gwen frowned thoughtfully. "Although with age I see that he wasn't bad. He just had no reason to care for me."

"Aside from being your father?" Olivia asked in an arch tone. She'd had years of fallout with her father too, so Gwen knew it was a sensitive subject for her, too.

"He isn't my father." The absolute silence made her smile. "My mother had affairs, and I'm the result of one of them."

"Affairs? Plural?" Eve looked at her teacup. "We may need something stronger to put in this."

"Do you know who your father is?" Olivia asked.

"I'm not sure it matters," she said, knowing that it did a little.

Eve shook her head. "You're a living soap opera. I can see how you wouldn't want any of that getting out. I can also see how it'd produce a toxic environment at home."

"I left for more than that. I always had to act in a way befitting an heiress. Everyone was always judging. My family, their acquaintances, the media." She leaned forward. "I'm *not* an heiress."

"No, you're not," Olivia said with a gentle smile.

"Unless heiresses go around with paint smeared on their faces," Eve added. "Then you'd totally be one."

She lifted her hand to her face automatically, even though she knew she couldn't have any paint on her. She hadn't been to the store since the story broke.

Olivia reached for a cookie. "So you're out of the closet. What's next? Has your family contacted you?"

She shook her head. "I haven't been at the store because of all reporters, and no one knows where I live. But it's only a matter of time before they show up on my doorstep."

The door buzzed. She'd have been freaked out, but she knew it was Lola.

Her author friend bounded in a moment later. "What did I miss?"

"We were talking about what Gwen's going to do next," Eve said, holding out the plate of madeleines.

Lola took two. "I told her she needs a game changer."

"I'm just not sure what that is." She frowned into her tea. "For a second I thought about running away again, but I won't. I'm done letting my past dictate my future. I love it here. I love my life and my friends."

Eve sniffled, but it was Olivia who said, "We wouldn't let you go."

"I keep asking myself, what would my grandmother do?" She lifted her chin. "Mamie Yvette would have waved a jeweled hand and told people exactly how it was going to be."

"So have a press conference," Eve said.

They all looked at her.

She shrugged. "It's the best thing. The media is harassing you, so give them what they want and they'll grow bored with you. Right now, it's only because you're unavailable that they're interested. A press conference would nip it in the bud."

"She's right," Olivia said.

"I'll help you set it up." Eve smiled. "They used to pay me the big bucks to do that sort of thing."

"Even with a press conference, you'll never be completely incognito," Lola pointed out.

Olivia nodded. "But her infamy will be on her terms. She can use it to her advantage where she couldn't before. Like with the de Young commission."

"True," Gwen said, her mind racing at the possibilities. "I've felt such resentment lately for having to guard everything I do. I want to live out loud."

"Nothing's louder than a press conference." Eve sat up with a gasp. "*No.* Better yet, an exclusive interview. I wonder if we can get Diane Sawyer to do it. I'll look into it."

"I feel like I'm standing on a precipice. One side is safe, and the other is scary as hell." She grinned suddenly. "But the scary side is so much more exciting."

"That's decided." Olivia set down her mug and leaned back. "Now about Rick."

Lola perked up. "Is that the hot guy you pelted with a squash?"

Eve laughed. "You didn't."

"I did." Gwen deflated. "I blamed him for all of this, but I made a mistake. A *big* mistake. The reporter who did the article on the museum was responsible."

Olivia nodded. "Rick's upset that you didn't trust him."

"I can see that." She hugged her legs to herself, resting her chin on her knees. "I said awful things to him on top of it all."

Eve patted her arm. "He's a private detective.

He's the go-to guy for finding stuff out, of course you'd suspect him. It doesn't help that he's relentless in his pursuit for information."

"The question is, what are you going to do to fix it?" Olivia asked, her gaze direct and steady.

"I might be able to help," Lola said.

They all turned to her.

Her cheeks flushed. "Helping the heroine and hero get their happy ending is what I do for a living," she said modestly.

"Do you have a suggestion for what I can do?" Gwen asked.

"He's a private eye?"

"Of the highest order," Olivia replied with a dry smile.

Lola worried her lip, a distant look in her eyes. Then she grinned, big and brilliant. "I think I may have a plan."

Chapter Twenty-six

*T*HE PRESS CONFERENCE was exactly what Gwen thought it'd be: complete torture.

Eve offered Grounds for Thought as the location for it, arranging everything to perfection. She even advised Gwen on how to present herself, which was the only reason she was wearing Eve's high heels.

For a brief moment when she stepped into the café and in front of all the flashing cameras, she froze, overcome by the old claustrophobia. But then she heard Mamie Yvette whisper, *Be yourself, ma chère, and you will always succeed*.

So she lifted her head, sashayed into the room, and said, "The first person to make a pumpkin joke will have one thrown at his head, and I'm an excellent shot."

They all laughed, and the press conference began.

Half an hour into answering questions, Gwen looked up to find her uncle standing in a corner at the back. She faltered a moment, but then continued when she saw he was alone.

A rush of pleasure flowed through her, making her smile. She'd always loved Jacques. He'd always been fun and carefree where her father—his brother—had been dour and serious. Other than her grandmother, he'd been the only one who'd ever shown her caring.

She wasn't sure how long she'd fielded questions, but finally Eve stepped up and told the crowd to help themselves to refreshments. Gwen gave Eve a hug and dodged the crowd to look for her uncle.

She found him outside on the patio, alone, sitting on a bench smoking a Gauloises. She smiled at the familiarity of it—the cigarette, the relaxed sprawl. The only thing that was different was the gray in his hair and the lines on his face.

Even aged, Jacques de la Roche still looked like the playboy he'd always been.

Stepping outside, she closed the door behind her.

He smiled in that way that wrapped women around his pinkie. Dropping the cigarette, he stood and held his arms out. "*Geneviève, ma petite*."

"It's Gwendolyn now," she said as she let him kiss her cheeks.

"You were always the most impossible child," he said affectionately, switching to English. "I'm glad to see that hasn't changed. Sit."

She sat next to him, feeling an odd mix of distance and time and longing. "I was sad to hear about Mamie Yvette."

"It was a great loss." A look of sadness swept over his face. "*Maman* missed you, you know."

Why did she have a feeling his sadness was feigned? "I missed her, too," she said cautiously.

"We all hoped you'd return for her funeral. When you didn't, we feared the worse." He arched a brow at her and pulled out another Gauloises from an engraved cigarette case. "Your mother misses you, as well."

She resisted the urge to roll her eyes at that. Her mother only missed seeing the live reflection of herself. "How is she?"

"Janine? Ageless." He lit his cigarette. "You look so much like her. Except for your hair, no? That is all you."

Her curls had always been a sore subject. Her mother used to insist on having "that unfortunate hair" straightened. "And Gautier?"

"Your father is as always." He smiled deprecatingly. "It's why I'm here."

Frowning, she shook her head. "I don't understand."

"Over the years, he and I haven't seen eye to eye." Jacques took a casual drag off the cigarette, blowing the smoke up and away from her. "We disagree about the way the company is run. While *Maman* was alive, she kept Gautier from running unchecked, but now that she's gone..."

She waited for him to continue, suspecting she knew where this was going and feeling sad about it. "Now that she's gone?"

He shrugged in the way only the French did. "I want to keep the company as *Maman* wanted it, but Gautier has other ideas. Disastrous ones. He wants to cut costs and corners to increase profits, regardless of sacrificing quality. And Roger, you know he does as your father wishes."

"That's Roger."

"Yes, and together they have control of the company."

She stilled, waiting, hoping she was wrong about the reason he was there. That he'd simply missed her. She waited for to see how long it'd be before he asked her.

But she wasn't wrong. Jacques took her hand. "If you sign control of your shares to me, I'll at least have an equal share. I'll be able to keep *Maman*'s vision alive."

The disappointment was soft, like a little breeze that brought a whiff of something spoiled with it. It was too good to be true, hoping that he'd come just because he'd missed her. That wasn't the way her family operated.

"I know you know nothing of the de la Roche Corporation, Geneviève. Gwendolyn," he corrected himself with a wry grin. "You've never expressed any interest in the running of it. Then why should you shoulder those responsibilities? And I read you're an accomplished artist now."

"I am."

"All the more reason to give the shares to someone who will safeguard them and your beloved grandmother's vision for the company, is it not? Before Gautier and Roger try to wrest your shares from you."

Kate Perry

She tried to picture that scenario. She wouldn't put it past her father, but her brother? They had never been close, but he had a good heart. He'd never willingly screw someone over. That she believed with every fiber of her being.

"Geneviève, you cannot tell me you want Gautier to get your shares. He doesn't deserve them." Jacques leaned forward, his regard conspiratorial. "Especially since he isn't your father. Better give them to your real father, no?"

She gaped, unable to speak. Finally she croaked, "You?"

He took her hand. "I'm sorry I haven't been able to acknowledge you all these years. Janine didn't want me to rock the boat. Ridiculous considering Gautier knew all along."

"He knew it was you?" she asked, as horrified understanding dawned.

"Janine made sure he knew." Jacques smiled sadly. "Why else would she have had the affair with me? She wanted to stab him where it would hurt most. What better way than to have a child with me? It is the ultimate revenge, is it not?"

It all fell into place: why her dad, who was really her uncle, hated her but hadn't cast her out; why her mother was so smug; why her grandmother still loved her so much even when she knew she wasn't her father's child. That she was Jacques's child made everything fit into place. He was Mamie Yvette's favorite—despite his flaws, Mamie Yvette used to say.

When she'd been younger, she remembered wishing that her uncle were really her father. He'd been so much nicer, bringing her little toys all the time all .

The toys had occupied her—to keep her busy while *he* was busy with Janine? Gwen didn't know what to think—to feel.

She cleared the emotion from her throat. "So you knew I was your daughter all along?"

He smiled deprecatingly. "Janine made no effort to hide it."

She had from Gwen. "But you didn't want to claim me out in the open?"

He blinked. "I couldn't. Think of the paparazzi. It would have destroyed our company."

"The company." She nodded. Of course. "And now?"

"Now?" He frowned. "Now you come back to the family. And you sign your shares to me so I can protect them."

"And you and me?"

He shrugged expressively. "What do you want me to promise you, Geneviève? The fairy tales Maman used to tell you?"

"Yes."

"I cannot."

She nodded, not surprised but still let down. Although she wasn't as saddened as she expected to be, probably because she knew one man who could offer her a happy-ever-after.

She stood up. "My answer is no."

"No?" He uncrossed his legs. "You cannot —"

"This conversation is over." She headed to the door, pausing when she touched the handle. Looking over her shoulder, she said, "For the record, you'd have been a better father, at least for as long as I was useful."

"That's unfair," he says.

"Life is unfair," she said, quoting Gautier. "Get over it."

"You make a mistake, Geneviève," Jacques called.

"You're the one who made the mistake, Jacques, by assuming I'm Janine's and your daughter."

"But of course you are."

"No." She shook her head. "I'm Yvette de la Roche's granddaughter."

She swore she could hear her grandmother clap for her as she left the patio.

Eve met her with worried eyes and a glass of champagne. "I didn't know where you went. Are you alright?"

"I'm perfect." She took the champagne, saluted up toward her grandmother's perch in Heaven, and downed the whole glass.

"Okay, then." Eve refilled her glass. "You're doing okay. Good."

"Except for your shoes. They're killing me." She shifted her weight from foot to foot. "How do you wear them all day?"

"There's a price to looking fabulous."

The price was too high for her. She was taking them off first opportunity. After she took care of one little detail. "Can I use your kitchen for a phone call, Eve?"

"Of course." Her friend waved her away. "Go ahead."

Nodding, she strode into the kitchen, pulling her

phone out of the hidden pocket of her full skirt. It took a moment to connect overseas, and then another minute to get past the receptionist and five assistants to the person she wanted.

There was a second of disbelieving silence when he came on the line. Then he said, "Geneviève?"

"Hello, Roger." She took a deep breath. "We need to talk, please."

Chapter Twenty-seven

IT WAS A sea of people, none of whom Camille knew.

She did recognize some of them from her mother's parties, but she was usually flying so far under the radar that none of them remembered her. But tonight they were all here for her—to celebrate her triumph.

She hated it.

She hated the people and how they were all fake. She hated the way they groveled and kissed her mother's ass. She hated the hubris that radiated from them.

Elizabeth was eating it up, though. She flitted proudly from group to group, sipping her wine and smoking her cigarette, greeting everyone with a falseness that set Camille's teeth on edge.

Had this scene always been so superficial? Or

was it just because she had comparison between the genuine caring Gwendolyn had shown her.

She nibbled the edge of her nail, looking around for Dylan. He'd promised to come tonight. At least in an email. She could tell from the tone of the email he hadn't been excited about it, but he'd promised, so she knew he'd show up.

She missed Dylan.

He hadn't talked to her since he'd called to give her his CIA contact's information. She knew he was disappointed in her. Truthfully, she knew where he was coming from. She was disappointed in herself.

But she was going to change things. Starting with tonight.

If—*when* he showed up.

"Camille." Elizabeth swooped down on her, frowning. "Stop biting your nails and come meet my friend, Jason Craven. He's the publisher at Hyde Street Books."

She let her suddenly proud mother drag to meet the guy. At first glance, he looked skeezy, like he was only there hoping to score with her mother, which had a high ick factor.

He shook her hand, too enthusiastically. "I didn't

realize Elizabeth had a daughter."

She wanted to assure him no one else attending tonight did either, but then she saw Dylan's head and all other thoughts flew from her mind.

The entire evening transformed. Suddenly she felt like she had space within her to breathe.

Then she noticed the tall blonde next to him. She couldn't miss the woman, not in that flaming red dress that hugged all of her long sleek curves. Camille would have dismissed her except that Dylan put his hand on her back.

The blonde shifted closer to him, smiling the kind of private smile you gave your lover.

Intimate.

"Camille, you're dripping on me," her mother's harsh voice cut into her misery.

She looked down to see that her drink was tipping over. She murmured something and returned her attention to Dylan and the blonde, in time to see him kiss her cheek and walk to the bar.

He'd gone to get his date a drink.

He brought a *date*. To *her* party.

It was like a cold splash of water on her face.

Camille tried to think about it rationally. She

hadn't told him he couldn't bring someone. It wasn't like they had *that* sort of relationship—they'd never actually had that date.

Her fault.

Then why did it feel like he'd betrayed her a little bit? And why did she feel this angry hopelessness, like she was about to lose something more important than anything she'd ever wanted?

Her mother's laugh jarred her out of the moment. The sound was abrasive. Too loud. She looked over at her. Elizabeth wore head-to-toe black, cigarette in one hand, drink in the other. She was smiling, but her eyes were flat.

Camille blinked. Were her mother's eyes always like that? She looked...

Unpleasant was the word that came to mind.

Was that what she wanted to become? It made her feel itchy and uncomfortable on the inside.

What Gwen had said to her had weighed heavily the past few days. Camille had been rethinking everything, really thinking about what she wanted out of life. If she could be free and be anything or anyone?

She'd write stories that made people *feel*, not articles no one cared about.

Dylan had been right.

Only she hadn't said anything—to anyone—because she didn't want to rock the boat. Elizabeth had arranged this party, and she hadn't wanted to upset her mother. And when she tried calling Dylan, he hadn't answered the phone. She'd figured she'd have time to tell him tonight.

But then he showed up with that blonde...

Scared that she'd messed something up, Camille shoved her glass at a waiter passing by and charged for Dylan. She'd tell him, and everything would work out.

He turned right as she approached him, as if he sensed her. Before he could say anything, she surprised them both by grabbing his collar and kissing him.

When they finally parted, he looked dazed and confused.

That made two of them. She touched her lips, which still tingled. She'd had boyfriends since she was in high school, but she'd never been kissed like that, and Dylan had been ambushed. How would he kiss when he was completely into it? She licked her lip, imagining.

His gaze flicked to her mouth. "Camille?"

Right. There was time for daydreaming—and more—later. "I need to talk to you."

"That was an interesting way of opening a conversation."

"That's what I want to talk about." She stepped closer, pushing her nerves aside, and put a hand on his sleeve.

Dylan squeezed her hand and then lifted it from his arm. "Tonight's not a good time."

"You were right," she said quickly, knowing that if she didn't say it all now, the moment would be lost—Dylan would be lost to her. "You were right about everything. About Elizabeth, about my writing, about my career. I should have listened to you."

He nodded solemnly. "You should have."

She heaved a deep breath. "But I'm listening now. I'm listening to everything now."

He stared at her. Then he glanced over her head.

She looked behind her shoulder. The blonde watched them warily, question and confusion in her eyes. "Who is she?"

"Lola? A friend of mine. She's an author," he added.

And probably super-successful. Camille felt both

jealous and guilty simultaneously. She didn't want to hurt the woman, but neither was she going to back off. She faced Dylan again.

He was staring at her. For once, she could read his expression, and it didn't bode well for her.

"I'm sorry, Camille," he said finally. He squeezed her arm and walked to the blonde.

Camille turned, watching him walk away. He took the blonde's hand and said something to her as he led her out of the bar.

Camille hadn't known he'd held her heart until that very moment when she let him hand it back to her.

"*Camille*." Her mother's talons gripped her arm. There was a smile on Elizabeth's face, but her eyes were cold with displeasure. "This is an important night for your career and you're underperforming. You need to focus."

"I'm going home."

She wasn't sure who was most startled: her or Elizabeth. But her mother recovered first. "You can't go home. If you leave, you might as well quit being a journalist."

"Okay." She turned to leave.

Elizabeth grabbed her arm. "What are you doing, Camille? Is this some stupid plea for my attention?"

"If I wanted your attention I'd keep backstabbing people who've been nice to me and publish stories about them in the paper." She extracted her arm. "But I don't have the stomach to do that, even if it means you won't love me."

Elizabeth blinked but didn't say anything.

Tell me you love me. Camille waited, mentally urging her mother for something—any little acknowledgement. But it didn't come. She wanted to kiss her mother's cheek and tell her it was okay—that she understood—but she really didn't. She just felt sad.

"Thank you for the party," she said politely, wishing she could say *I love you. Please love me too.*

If wishes were horses, she thought as she watched her mother whirl and return to her adoring friends.

Chapter Twenty-eight

LOLA'S IDEA SUCKED.

Gwen tugged the tight skirt down for the hundredth time. She was sure she flashed at least half a dozen people as she got out of the cab. Why would they think she'd be okay in a dress that was shorter than most shirts, much less heels so high?

Granted, she looked fantastic. Her body looked like it had curves that'd make the autobahn jealous. The red dress was tight and left little to the imagination. She had her hair pulled back into an elegant twist, and there was more paint on her face than on some of her gourds.

She wasn't wearing underwear.

Taking a deep breath, she strode with determination, up the two flights of stairs, down the hall, to the entrance of Clancy Private Investigators. She stopped in front of it, her hand on the doorknob.

What if it didn't work?

Lola had assured her it would. The heroine always got the hero in the end, her friend said, as long as the hero really loved her.

That was the part she wasn't sure of. Olivia assured her he did, but you could love someone and be in denial.

Or it could have been about the sex, which, admittedly, had been fantastic.

Or he could have decided she wasn't worth the trouble.

"Stop," she hissed at herself. She opened the door and strutted in like she owned the world.

Technically, she did.

Mamie Yvette had left her more than her fair share of the de la Roche Corporation. When Gwen had talked to her brother, he'd told her that Jacques wanted to sell the company and all its subsidiaries to another conglomerate, and that he and Gautier were the only thing keeping it from happening.

Did she have proof that what Roger said was true? No. But she instinctively believed his version of the story.

She'd given him controlling rights to her shares

outright. There wasn't a doubt in her mind that Mamie Yvette would have wanted that.

She'd actually *talked* with Roger, for the first time ever. It'd felt good. She'd told him about her life and her art. She'd even mentioned Rick, and how she'd messed things up but was going to rectify it. Roger had told her he had every confidence in her. Apparently he'd met a divorcee who he wanted to marry. Janine and Gautier didn't approve of her, of course. Roger said he didn't care. Loving was rare, he'd said, and when you found it you held on with both fists.

That was what she was doing.

She closed the door behind her. Then she locked it, just to be safe.

"Hello?"

His voice gave her goose bumps of anticipation, right along the jangle of nerves in her belly.

She could do this. Nodding, she walked into his office and leaned in the doorway, the way Lola had told her to do. "I want to hire Sam Spade," she said in an especially husky voice.

He didn't say anything.

At first she didn't notice, she was so happy to see him. He looked tired but so...

So *hers*.

But then it registered that he was watching her with a guarded look. She was starting to get worried when he said, "Sam's taken."

"And you?" she said, hoping she sounded hot instead of desperate like she felt.

He leaned back, his long legs stretched on his desk. "Depends."

She leaned in, knowing her dress was riding up her legs. "I think I've something that'd interest you."

"Really."

She stepped into the office and her ankle turned. *"Fille de bordelle,"* she yelled as she grabbed for a chair to steady herself.

Something in her snapped. She felt the rage of having to hide herself for so many years, the disapproval and ridicule from so many people.

That was it. From this point, she was going forward the way she wanted, to hell with what anyone thought. Even Rick Clancy—because if he couldn't love her for who she really was, then he wasn't right for her.

"Are you okay?" Rick asked, standing up.

"No, I'm not." Scowling, she waved at herself.

"This isn't me."

He arched a brow. "It's not?"

"No, of course it isn't, and you know it. Stick a fork in me, I'm *done*." She toed off her shoes and kicked them to the side with a sigh of relief. Then she lowered her head and began pulled at the pins, dropping them on the floor. When she thought she probably had them all out, she shook out her carefully coiffed hair.

Then she wiped the crimson lipstick off with the back of her hand. She faced him, boiling with anger. "*This* is me. This, and the gourds, and the roller-blades."

His brow furrowed. "Gwendolyn —"

"*No*." She held out to forestall him. "I'm laying it all out, so there's no question of what I'm offering here. You claimed that I hid from you, but you're wrong. Everything you saw was the real me. Geneviève de la Roche never existed except in the minds of my parents and the media."

Eyes narrowed, she stalked toward him. "The real me is Gwen, the crazy woman who draws on pumpkins and rollerblades in the rain. She wears color, not black, and she has friends who care about her, not her bank account or that she owns half the world. She steals into neighbor's backyards—"

"I thought you said you had a key," he said.

"Shut up." She pointed at him. "I'm not done."

"Sorry."

She took a breath to take up where she left off, but she couldn't remember where that was. She threw her hands in the air, pacing. "*Great*. You've made me forget my point."

"I think I can help you with that." He came around his desk.

And stopped right in front of her. "There's just one thing," he said.

"What?" she asked softly.

He lowered his head and kissed her.

Only it wasn't just a kiss. It was anger and retribution. It was love and forgiveness.

It was a promise. A vow.

She clung to his shirt, pressing herself against him, hungry for him. "I missed you," she murmured against his lips.

He nodded, moving her backwards onto his desk.

Some things skittered to the floor. She reached behind her to brace herself and forced herself to break away from his kiss, wrenching as it was. "I was being serious."

"How serious?"

She frowned. "As serious as I can get."

"If that means 'till death do us part,' then we're on the same page."

She stilled. "What?"

"I love you, Gwendolyn Geneviève-de-la-Roche Pierce." He held her chin. "I love you regardless of the colors you wear, but especially when you wear bright orange and nothing else. I love how you turn vegetables into an art form. I love the way you care about other people, even annoying teenagers. I love your sense of recklessness, even when I want to throttle you. I love how you pranced in here in that little red dress, making me so hot, and then turning the tables on me by engaging my heart at the same time."

He lifted her face to his. "I love you, Gwendolyn, pure and simple."

"Oh." She blinked.

"Oh?" He arched his brow.

She shrugged. "That was really nice."

"And?"

"Yes." She nodded. "It means 'till death do us part.'"

He narrowed his beautiful gaze. "I plan on being alive a very long time."

"Good, because I'm not going anywhere."

"Good," he said, too, "because I feel like I've been looking for you all my life."

"Yes," she agreed, and she pulled his mouth down to hers and took him. Forever.

Chapter Twenty-nine

CAMILLE FOUND HIM at Four Barrels, sitting in his usual spot in the window, sun beaming down on him, intently tapping at his computer.

Her heart caught in her throat. It'd been weeks since the night of her party. She hadn't seen or heard from him since.

Dylan looked like he always did: focused and intense. He wore jeans and a black T-shirt that hugged his muscular shoulders. He impatiently pushed back the lock of hair that always flopped on his forehead and resumed typing.

She felt the flutter she always did when she saw him, but this time she knew what that flutter meant: that she wanted him. Wholly and completely, for always.

If only she hadn't blown it.

She swallowed her misery. It was too late — she'd

accepted that, and one day she'd get over it. Maybe. Sure, she'd held out hope but when he didn't return her calls after a couple weeks, she knew she'd blown it irreparably.

But that wasn't why she was here.

He looked up and stared straight at her.

Now or never. Lifting her shoulders, she strode toward him.

"This is unexpected," Dylan said, turning away from his laptop.

She tried not to be hurt that he didn't hug her hello, or kiss her cheek. She tried not to notice that he didn't sound especially thrilled to see her.

Taking a deep breath, she held out the stack of papers she held in her arm. "This is for you."

He just stared at it, making no move to take it. "What is it?"

"My book." She shrugged. "Well, half my book. I haven't finished it yet."

"Why are you giving it to me?"

Because he'd inspired it. Because she loved him. "Because I thought you might be able to give me feedback."

She held it out, steadily, even though she was

shaking inside. Was he going to take it?

"What's it about?" he asked, reaching out to accept it.

She sighed in relief. "It's about a teenage girl on the wrong track and the boy who's waiting for her in the wings."

He looked up at her sharply. "You're writing a young adult book?"

"It felt right."

"Yes." He set the partial manuscript next to his computer. "It's perfect actually. You're clever to realize it."

She was anything but clever, she wanted to tell him. Instead, she said, "The boy is her best friend, but the heroine doesn't realize that she's in love with him for way too long."

"That's a good conflict," Dylan said, crossing his arms. "I bet the boy is incredibly patient, even though the girl acts very stupidly. Very, *very* stupidly."

Camille frowned. "She's not *that* stupid."

He reached out and tugged her into his arms. "But I bet the boy would be willing to forgive her stupidity."

Impossible hope flared in her chest. She looked

up into his dear eyes. "Would he? Even if she didn't deserve it?"

"She deserves it," he said softly. "He's always thought so."

And then he kissed her.

She'd been right—when he was focused on the kissing it was dark and delicious. Addictive. Toe-curling.

Perfect.

He lifted his head. "How is your story going to end?"

She touched his face. "I'm shooting for a happy ever after."

More Laurel Heights Books by Kate

Perfect for You (Laurel Heights #1)

Graphic designer looking for hot sex.

Freya Godwin shook her head and crossed out the sentence. Too blatant. That may be what she was looking for, but maybe she should be a touch more subtle. She didn't want every freak in San Francisco to respond to her ad.

Doodling faceless lovers entwined in different passionate embraces, she thought about what she really wanted. Finally she scribbled:

> *Female web designer seeking inspiration in*
> *order to complete a very important project.*
> *Bring your muse to share.*

Lame. Accurate, sure, but it sounded desperate. Who was she kidding? She was totally desperate.

Her office door slammed open. Flinching, she looked up to find Charles scowling in the threshold.

Hell. She quickly flipped the notebook shut. If he knew she was spending her valuable time working on a personal ad instead of the Sin City redesign, he'd blow a gasket.

"What the hell is this?" He waved sheets of paper in the air.

Maybe he'd blow a gasket anyway. "I can't see the pages with you flapping them around like that."

He strode into her office and slammed them on her desk. "Here."

Freya glanced down and mentally winced. The design was even more white bread than she remembered. She didn't need Charles to tell her that Sin City wasn't shelling out the big bucks for white bread—they were paying for buttery French pastry.

"Well? What the hell is this crap?"

It was the last throes of a web designer who hadn't felt an iota of creativity in over a year. But she just shrugged. "They're some initial ideas I had. They're not the final mock ups to show the client."

"Damn right, they aren't. If they saw this"—he stabbed a blunt finger at the printouts—"they'd run out of the building in horror. This is crap."

"Tell me what you really think, Charles."

Ignoring her, he braced his hands on the desk and leaned forward. "Do you understand what a coup it was for them to choose Evolve to redesign their website and revamp their branding?"

Yeah, she did. Evolve was well regarded in San Francisco's competitive web design field, but to call Sin City hiring Evolve a coup was understating matters. It was unheard of for a huge corporate entity like Sin City to go outside the biggie web design firms to a boutique shop like Evolve.

And Sin City was huge. They were Amazon and Facebook combined but for all things sexual. Store, blogs, chats, reviews, live video feeds—you name it. They even had their own publishing branch that put out several magazines in addition to a line of erotica for women. Compared to Sin City, the Playboy empire looked like a business run out of someone's garage.

"They didn't just choose Evolve, Freya." Charles's blue eyes burned with the zeal he was renowned for among his colleagues. His employees called it The Mania. "They chose you."

Because of the site she'd designed for a local sex toy shop two years ago. Back before her creative juices had dried up. "I understand, Charles."

"I'm not sure you do. If you screw this up, you're out of here."

Her mouth fell open. It took a couple tries before she could get any words out. "You can't fire me for one bombed design."

"I'm the boss. I can do whatever the hell I want. Especially if one of my employees blows the biggest opportunity this company has ever had." His eyes sparked with dollar signs. "This is our opportunity to play with the big boys. Maybe even go public. I won't let anyone screw it up."

"But—"

"And your work over the past year hasn't been up to your usual standards. I know Marcus bailed you out of the Accordiana job," he said bluntly.

She cut off her protest. She couldn't deny it— Marcus hadn't just helped her out with the design, he'd taken the crap she'd come up with and turned it into gold.

"If you can't perform, I can't afford to keep you. Just because you're Evangeline's best friend doesn't mean I'm going to make allowances for you."

"I can't lose my job." Her stomach lurched at the thought.

"Then I suggest you produce a design they fall in love with." He snapped his suit coat straight and turned to leave. At the door he looked over his shoulder. "I mean it, Freya. Fuck this up and you're out of here."

She winced as the door slammed shut. She couldn't afford to lose her job. It wasn't that she cared about herself—if she lost her paycheck she'd figure something out. But she wouldn't be able to support her sister Anna through college, and that wasn't acceptable. She'd vowed after the fallout from her parents' accident that Anna would never have to compromise her dreams like she'd had to.

That meant she had to produce a kick-ass design.

In the pit of her stomach she felt a spasm of worry. She'd been off her game—she'd never felt such an utter lack of creativity.

She grabbed the notebook and opened it to her ad. She crossed it out and wrote

Artist in trouble. HELP.

Close to You (Laurel Heights #2)

Like every morning in the six months since she'd opened Grounds for Thought, Eve Alexander peeked from the kitchen window to check on her bookstore café. Gleaming espresso machine. Sparse stacks of books specially showcased through the inviting space. People drinking and reading.

Her dream come true.

And, like every morning, she had the same thought. She was *insane*.

Shaking her head, she picked up a tray of hot scones and carried it out to the front, careful not to get her heels caught on the knotty wood flooring.

Her friends teased her for wearing her impractical fancy shoes in the café but a girl had to have standards. Besides, she loved them—and she had a backup pair of flip-flops in the kitchen in case her feet began to hurt badly.

"Watch out," Eve warned her barista Allison.

The older woman stepped out of the way and inhaled deeply. "Clotted cream and orange. If I outgrow my wardrobe, you'll have to give me a raise."

"You deserve a raise regardless." Eve set the scones to cool on a rack strategically placed so customers could see and smell them. "I don't know what I'd do without you."

"The word *whimper* comes to mind."

"No kidding." Eve couldn't afford to have someone else on staff yet, but Allison had offered to work for practically nothing, just to have something to do other than watching TV and gardening. Having Allison saved her from working twenty-four/seven but, even better, offered her friendship. "How's it going out here?"

"It's been steady this morning. People seem really interested in the book club. We're going to need more flyers."

"Great," she said, perking up. She'd started the book club two months ago, to pull more revenue in. Last month she had eighteen attendees—eighteen people who bought not only the book they were discussing but also drinks and pastries. This month she was hoping to double attendance.

"The idea you had to do a singles night is excellent too," Allison said. "God knows it's hard to meet anyone unless you hang out in a bar."

"What do you know about dating?"

"I may be happily married, but a lot of my friends are getting divorced and starting over. They talk, sometimes too much. Unlike you."

"I don't have anything to talk about."

"My point exactly." Her barista got a calculating look in her eyes. "I hear online dating is all the rage."

"My best friend Freya did that, and don't even *think* about putting up a profile for me behind my back."

Allison exhaled. "Killjoy."

Her cell phone rang, and Eve reached into her apron pocket to answer it. The glow from Allison's praise melted away when Eve saw it was Charles on the phone. She groaned. "I have to take this."

The older woman shooed her away. "Go talk in the kitchen. I'm fine out here."

Nodding glumly, she waited until she was in the

kitchen and out of Allison's hearing to answer. "Hey Dad. What's going on?"

"I got your check for this month's rent. It was late."

"It should have only been a day late."

"Late is late, Evangeline."

She put a hand to her temple. She'd thought it was bad when her father was her boss—it was ten times worse having him as her landlord. "I missed the mail deadline and sent it a day later than I meant to. I'm sorry. Next time I'll just drop it off."

"You can't go around stiffing money to your business partners."

"Dad, I didn't stiff you money. I just—"

"I knew this store of yours was a bad idea," he continued, speaking over her. "You work all the time and are in debt up to your eyeballs."

"It's not *that* bad." It was, but he didn't know it. He thought she'd invested all her savings. She hadn't told him that she'd taken a second mortgage on her condo too. And there was no way in hell she was telling him that she was thirty days from bankruptcy.

"It was a mistake to encourage you by leasing that property. I shouldn't have let you convince me."

She hadn't asked him to take the lease out for her—it'd been his idea to lease it and rent it to her. But she wasn't sure she would have qualified for it on her own, so she went along with it.

Mistake. Big mistake.

Return to You (Laurel Heights #3)

"You want me to *what*?"

Everett Parker would have smiled if he were that kind of man. But he wasn't, so he patiently watched and waited. He was excellent at waiting, and even better at getting what he wanted.

"This is a joke, right?" The young man swept his hand through his hair. "Well, it's not funny."

Leaning back in his leather chair, Parker took a sip of his scotch before answering, aware of the tension he was causing. "No joke, Michael. You heard correctly the first time. I want you to shoot the film in Mill Valley."

"Shit." The director speared his fingers through his hair again and started to pace.

Parker nursed his drink, watching him coolly.

Once Michael's tantrum ran dry, he'd do what he was told. After all, the terms of the offer would be irresistible.

I'll make sure of that.

It was almost a shame he had to do this. He admired the young man. Of all the people around him, Michael Wallace was the only one who stood up to him. The rest of them cowered in corners, peeing on themselves as he walked by.

He wasn't manipulated easily, something Parker usually relished. At this moment, it irritated him. He needed Michael's cooperation, but he'd never consent of his own free will—meaning Parker was going to have to force him. Not easy, but certainly not impossible. He just had to find the right bargaining chip. "Sit down."

Glaring, Michael dropped into the guest chair. To his credit, he remained silent, though his heated eyes said enough.

Good boy, Parker thought, feeling paternal pride even though Michael wasn't tied to him in any way other than business.

Which was what he intended to remedy. "You're the hottest director in the business. You can't be surprised I want you to direct *Love Unbound*."

The corner of Michael's lips quirked. "That wasn't what surprised me, and you know it. Stop playing games, Parker."

Once upon a time, the boy had called him Everett.

One more thing he had to set right.

Parker pushed aside the nostalgic thoughts so untypical of him and got back to the matter at hand. "Mill Valley is not only the perfect backdrop for the movie, the town is working with us to supply permits. It's as simple as that."

"There are dozens of little towns in California that would be just as suitable."

"I want the movie shot in Mill Valley."

Michael leaned forward, brimming with repressed intensity. "Why? What does Mill Valley have that can't be found anywhere else?"

My daughter. "Mill Valley is the most picturesque of quaint California towns."

"Since when?"

"Since it had a complete facelift a few years ago."

"Mill Valley would need more than a facelift to improve it. It'd need complete reconstructive surgery."

"Most of the filming will be done outside Mill Valley. At Pembroke Farm."

"Oh, *hell* no." The young man shook his head vehemently. "There is no fucking way. I can't go back to Pembroke Farm. Even you must see that."

"Enough," Parker said quietly. Most people froze in fear when they heard his low, menacing tone.

Michael was an exception. "No, it's not enough. I want to know why it's imperative to shoot this film there."

"Because I say it's imperative."

"Get some other director to do it then. How about Blasdell? He's up-and-coming and needs a break."

"I want you to direct."

"And if I say no?"

Parker cocked a brow in mock astonishment. "What about your contract with Parker Pictures?"

"I'll break it."

"Break it and you'll never work in this industry again."

"Damn it, Parker. What the hell is your game?"

"No game." With the instincts of a seasoned predator, he moved in for the kill. "I want *you* to direct this movie. I'll make any provisions I see fit and you'll follow them, just like your contract says. In return, once this movie is wrapped up, I'll release you from your contract."

Michael looked up sharply. "What?"

Everyone had a weak point. Find it, and they were yours. "You heard me."

"I want it in writing."

"I wouldn't have expected anything less."

The young man stared at him through narrowed eyes, fingers tapping rhythmically on his thigh. "Why don't I believe it's going to be that easy?"

"It will be." Parker sipped his scotch and waited.

"Isn't it too early in the day for that?" Michael asked out of the blue.

"It's never too early for fifty year single-malt."

He propped his elbows on his knees and rested his chin on his steepled hands. "Jesus, Parker. Does *she* know?"

About Kate

Kate has tangoed at midnight with a man in blue furry chaps, dueled with flaming swords in the desert, and strutted on bar tops across the world and back. She's been kissed under the Eiffel Tower, had her butt pinched in Florence, and been serenaded in New Orleans. But she found Happy Ever After in San Francisco with her Magic Man.

Kate's the bestselling author of the Laurel Heights Novels, as well as the Family and Love and Guardians of Destiny series. She's been translated into several languages and is quite proud to say she's big in Slovenia. All her books are about strong, independent women who just want love.

Most days, you can find Kate in her favorite café, working on her latest novel. Sometimes she's wearing a tutu. She may or may not have a jeweled dagger strapped to her thigh...

29012888R00181

Made in the USA
Lexington, KY
09 January 2014